UNTANGLING
TANGLEVILLE

THE SEQUEL

STEPPING OUT!
JUST AS ANY TOWN CAN

DONALD H. HULL

FriesenPress

Suite 300 - 990 Fort St
Victoria, BC, V8V 3K2
Canada

www.friesenpress.com

ISBN
978-1-5255-0971-1 (Hardcover)
978-1-5255-0972-8 (Paperback)
978-1-5255-0973-5 (eBook)

1. FICTION, CHRISTIAN

Distributed to the trade by The Ingram Book Company

How often do we focus on our differences rather than celebrating what we have in common? What positive change can occur when we bury hostility and small mindedness and seek common ground? Stepping Out is a tale of hope, the power of collaboration and the true meaning of community that answers these questions and provides a road map for those of us who want to live out our Christian values in this secular world. The message of the power of connectedness and principled action makes this book heart-warming, inspirational, and uplifting.

Martha Reavley, Ph.D., Professor of Management, Odette School of Business, University of Windsor.

My experience, whether in a small conversation, or within the context of a sermon given by Dr. Hull, has always left me saying "WOW" thereafter, and Dr. Hull's sequel to TANGLEVILLE does not disappoint. Canon Hull has penned a very thought-provoking, educational, and FACTional story, with that very "WOW" factor entangled throughout the book – it actually applies to anyone, in any town, anywhere.

Notwithstanding your convictions, be they religion based, secular, atheistic or agnostic, after reading this book, you will come away enlightened with the REALITY of today's society. You might even say "Dr. Hull has hit the proverbial nail right on the head! I urge anyone who has ever wondered, "What is this Christianity stuff anyway?" to take time to read THIS story.

Sharon A. Hillier, AScComm, BSc, LLC, retired.

Donald Hull has crafted a worthy follow-up to Tangleville, that takes the reader in unexpected and satisfying directions.

Peter Mudrack, Ph.D., Professor,
Kansas State University

Donald Hull once again presents a complex theological issue for us to grapple with and does so in the context of an engaging town with a wonderful cast of characters. For those who enjoyed Tangleville, you will be pleased to see the return of some favourite characters and enjoy introductions to some new ones. This second novel allows us to explore some difficult theological questions while enjoying the story of people attempting to do their best for their community, their church and their families. A most enjoyable read with a few surprises to ensure the book keeps you engaged until the very end.

Joyce Zuk, M.A., Executive Director
Family Services Windsor-Essex

FORWARD

If you were to untangle a tight knot, one that was getting tighter despite your efforts, who would you turn to for help? Someone with big fingers or someone with smaller fingers and a lighter touch? To phrase it differently, if you were the CEO of a growing conglomerate and your group of companies seemed to have lost direction where would you begin to turn things around? With the Board of Directors, the middle managers, or with the rank and file workers? If you were to consider Christianity to be a conglomerate, a large international company, how do you think God would untangle the twisted knot that Christianity seems to have become?

The Center for the Study of Global Christianity at Gordon-Conwell Seminary estimates that in 2012 there were some 43,000 Christian denominations. Some critics of Christianity love to argue that a true God couldn't be behind Christianity because a god would communicate better. This begs the question if one accepts that God is interested and concerned for its welfare, would God not use a strong hand of some sort, perhaps an all-out attack on Christianity, or perhaps a gentler movement to untangle the knotty situation that its critics point out that the Church that Jesus established has become?

Perhaps the change would come from an inspired clergy, something top-down, or perhaps the revitalization would come from rank and file Christians in the pews bottom-up. Jesus prayed to the Father that they be one and when accused of casting out devils from the sick, that he was doing it in the name of the Devil, he replied that a house divided against itself cannot stand. Christianity does seem to be in a state of upheaval faced with the increasing declining number of adherents and loss of influence and respect. Christianity certainly does not seem to be one and it certainly seems divided. Nor does it appear to know what the fix is. That is the sort of question that Donald Hull is attempting to address in his newest novel *Untangling Tangleville - Stepping Out! Just as Any Town Can.*

The main character of his first novel, *Tangleville, Just About Any Town Anywhere,* The Rev. Canon Dr. Barclay Steadmore is invited to return to his former parish of St. Bartholomew's for an anniversary service. In his sermon he issues a challenge to a Christian community that is living in an increasingly secular and sometimes hostile world. This challenge becomes the driving force of Hull's sequel: "Today we are a long, long way, as Christians, from being one in Christ." Then along with his wife Faith, he returns to resume his retirement in Trinity Harbour. Steadmore's challenge is taken up by his former crusty antagonist, the now-converted member of St. Bart's, Harry Sting, the host of the controversial talk show on AM KNOW radio. As he thinks about Steadmore's observation about Christian unity and varying Christian practices or expressions, Harry begins to formulate an idea. That idea provides the impetus for the plot of *Untangling Tangleville.* I'll give you a hint: "The Word of God is proclaimed by action."

I have known the Rev. Canon Doctor Donald H. Hull for some twenty years and have followed with interest his spiritual journey.

In fact, it was he who encouraged me to enter the Diaconate. From farm boy to high school math teacher, to United Church minister, to Anglican priest, to principal of Canterbury College in Windsor, Ontario, to university lecturer, to retirement and now to having written his second novel, it has been quite a journey. He has never lost his concern for social issues and the evolving role of the Church in a rapidly changing modern world. He has never shirked from asking the difficult questions. I remember one of his homilies in which he challenged the congregation, "If you were accused of being a Christian, would there be enough evidence to convict you?" That perhaps could be seen as a new spin on the question one might ask one's self to prepare for the Day of Judgment, but it is typical of Don Hull's probing mind. The allegorical sounding names of Barclay Steadmore, Harry Sting, Faith, Bishop Strickman, and Harriet Dearly, the social worker, might give a hint of Hull's thinking in *Untangling Tangleville*, but that you'll have to decide for yourself.

The Reverend Frederick Eldridge, M.A., Deacon and Spiritual Director

*To my spouse Faye, and the Mullins,
Livermore, and Armstrong families.
To be loved by all twelve is a gift from God.*

Acknowledgements

THERE are many to whom I owe thanks and appreciation for making this sequel possible:

To Thomas Smith, who served as editor and agent for my first novel: heartfelt thanks for your professional guidance. Your suggestions were greatly needed to round off the rough edges of my musings.

To Gillian Stefanczyk, who typed the manuscript: again I need to acknowledge that you are one of the few who can interpret my near-illegible handwriting.

To my spouse Faye, who endured my countless questions during the writing of this novel - questions such as, "What do you think of this idea," etc. Sometimes we agreed, sometimes we didn't!

* * *

Had I but served my God with half the zeal I served my kings,
He would not in mine age have left me naked to mine enemies.
Shakespeare, Henry VIII

Michel De Montaigne, in *Essays*, put it this way:

Man is certainly crazy. He could not make a mite,
and he makes gods by the dozen.

Untangling Tangleville is an attempt to prove both of the above quotations true.

INTRODUCTION

ST. Paul wrote in his Second Letter to Timothy:

> *For the time is coming when people will not put up with sound doctrine, but having itching ears, they will accumulate for themselves teachers to suit their own desires, and will turn away from listening to the truth and wander away to myths.* (2 Timothy 4:3-4)

In the preceding novel: *Tangleville: Just About Any Town Anywhere,* The Rev. Canon Dr. Barclay Stedmore's guest appearance on Harry Sting's morning radio show exposed St. Paul's warning about society turning from Christian values and practices producing a secular new religion.

It was a turning point in Sting's life as he came to grapple with his own faith convictions - or better put, lack of them - and subsequently was challenged to re-evaluate the message of Jesus Christ to the world. As a result, his life took on a new direction, and the novel dealt with his struggles and dreams of using his radio show to challenge his listeners to do the same.

Untangling Tangleville is the sequel to the above-mentioned novel, with Harry Sting taking the lead in attempting to challenge the various Christian denominations in Tangleville to work together as a co-operative, united witness to the non-religious secular residents of the fictional town.

Doors which were once locked to Christian influence opened one by one in ways which Harry could not have predicted. Denominations which were once insulated from one another began to break down their walls of theological isolation. Harry, the protagonist in the novel, discovers how ordinary committed people of faith can, if working together, bring about creative solutions to problems facing the church in modern secular society, proving the old adage: "If we don't work as one, the world will not listen." It is a proverb of unlimited possibilities.

Tangleville would never be the same again. The untangling process, once initiated, took on a life of its own!

CHAPTER ONE

HARRY Sting was lost in thought as he sat behind his desk at the Samaritan Inn. As director of the institution established as a domestic violence shelter for women, he found the position had increasingly consumed more and more of his time.

A few months following his acceptance of the position at the Samaritan Inn, he was appointed as the Communications Director for the Anglican Diocese of New Avondale, a role which the Bishop invited him to consider. Accepting the two positions meant that his former daily radio show timetable at AM KNOW had to be reduced to two weekly broadcasts: Monday and Thursday mornings. Harry's listening audience, in spite of his reduced air time, continued to grow.

The format of the show was now but a shadow of its previous iteration. In former times the Harry Sting Show, by design, was a daily one-hour broadcast that divided his audience into diametrically opposite camps. Harry would invite individual religious leaders and theological academics to be guests on his show, and then delight in belittling their faith positions by trumpeting secularism as the only reasonable lifestyle choice to be made in the twenty-first century. "Religion is for the weak and simple-minded," he would say.

The first half hour of each show was spent with Harry and his guest of the day sparring over theological concepts based on denominational doctrine, and then the second thirty minutes was a segment when there was the usual audience participation time of the show, when Harry delighted in stirring up the divided Tangleville community. Ratings for the show soared and Harry became one of the most admired (and hated) citizens of Tangleville. "I'm only doing my job," he would argue. After all, a radio station is a business enterprise.

Ratings were all that mattered.

Four years ago, everything changed when the Reverend Canon Doctor Barclay Steadmore, the rector of St. Bartholomew's Anglican Parish in Tangleville was invited to be a guest on the show. Harry finally had met his match! The listening audience was so mesmerized with the sparing couple that Doctor Steadmore became a frequently invited guest on the program.

In the meantime, unbeknown to the town, Harry and his wife Annie became close friends with Barclay and Faith Steadmore and the intervention of conscience became an issue. Both Sting and Steadmore came to the realization that hypocrisy was creeping into their lives as the façade of their perceived positions on the show were becoming more show business driven than exploring authentic faith proclamations. Harry experienced a religious conversion and became a member of St. Bartholomew's Anglican parish. As a result, the Harry Sting Show took on a new format, in which serious contemporary issues were thoughtfully examined. Religion was no longer ridiculed on the show, but was affirmed as a positive means by which to find solutions to secular society's 'anything goes' philosophy.

Harry's spouse, a devoted and faithful member of Tangleville's Russian Orthodox Parish, was an accomplished and wealthy artist in her own right. She had donated one hundred thousand dollars to initiate the building of the Samaritan Inn. Public donations quickly followed for its completion. The centre for abused women and addicts grew to a one hundred-bed facility. Now the center needed to rethink its future. Expansion of the facility was essential, as was as expanding its mandate in Tangleville.

Harry's position as Communications Director with the Diocese of New Avondale was becoming a means for him to be front and center in the denomination. Increasingly, Bishop Strickman was using Harry to handle the denomination's sometimes delicate and contentious issues with the secular media. Harry had become an expert in doing so and was relishing the challenge of promoting Christianity to the often times sceptical and hostile public.

Dr. Steadmore and Faith had moved away from Tangleville upon their retirement three years ago and the Reverend Canon Matthew Hudson became the new Rector of St. Bart's. Canon Hudson had made Dr. Steadmore an honourary assistant at the parish and in spite of the distance between Tangleville and Trinity Harbour, Barclay and Faith were often invited back to St. Bartholomew's with Dr. Steadmore preaching from the pulpit. Whenever Barclay and Faith were in town, the Stings and the Steadmores would meet for dinner, usually at the Red Pagoda Chinese Restaurant.

The sound of Harry's office telephone interrupted his musings as he sat at his desk at the Samaritan Inn. It was Annie on the other end.

"Am I interrupting anything important, Harry?" she enquired.

"No, glad you called! For the last few minutes or so I haven't accomplished anything constructive. I've been lost in thought of what has transpired in our lives over the past few years. So much change could never have been anticipated. Isn't that the way things happen when God is in control of one's life?"

"God works in mysterious ways," replied Annie. "But right now I need for you to do something on your way home for dinner tonight. Drop into the Chicken Shack and pick up two dinner boxes. Make mine white meat. I haven't had time to prepare dinner for tonight. Faith and I were out shopping this afternoon. We had lunch together and time just slipped away."

"It completely slipped my mind that Dr. Steadmore and Faith were to be in town," Harry replied. "I know that he's scheduled to preach at St. Bart's, but I forgot that it was this weekend. What do you say that we invite them to come for Sunday dinner and stay overnight with us?"

"That's such short notice for me, Harry. I can't have a Sunday dinner planned at this late date. You should have told me about this earlier in the week!"

"You're right, of course. Here's another suggestion. Call Faith and see if they can join us for dinner at the Red Pagoda. They can then bunk in with us for the night."

"I'll see if that will work for them. Don't forget to pick up the chicken dinners!"

Harry hung up the office telephone and smiled to himself. Over these thirty-five years of marriage, it had happened so many times. His spur-of-the-moment suggestions to Annie needed to be modified. She was the practical one. He was always thinking about creative opportunities, but she was the one with her feet firmly planted on the ground. He was the dreamer, the impulsive enthusiastic idealist. It's a mystery why opposites attract in marriage, he thought to himself.

Give and take. It is surely one of the foundation blocks of a successful marriage. The sooner one learns this after the wedding vows and rings are exchanged, fewer road blocks will surface down the road. If only the residents of the Samaritan Inn had been made aware of those principles before they'd arrived as guests.

It was already three thirty in the afternoon and Harry was nearing completion of his monthly report to the Board of Directors. If he set himself to the task, he knew that he could finish it before he left the office for the weekend.

At precisely three forty-five in the afternoon, Jean, the receptionist at the front desk, dialed Harry's desk.

"The police are here with a badly battered woman. You need to see her immediately!"

The report to the Board would have to wait. He hurried down the hall to the office of Harriet Dearly, the resident social worker. From Harriet's office the two waited for the female police officer and the crying young woman to enter. Harry knew he'd have to call Annie. The Friday evening chicken dinner was going to be a late event.

CHAPTER TWO

ANNIE called the Steadmores and invited them to spend the coming Sunday afternoon and night with her and Harry. It would be the perfect opportunity for the two couples to get together for dinner and an evening of celebrating old friendships. Faith and Barclay readily accepted and both were thoroughly looking forward to their return to St. Bart's.

The Sunday morning pews were packed. The rector, Canon Hudson, warmly welcomed Dr. Steadmore and Faith to the service. A reception in the parish hall was scheduled for a meet and greet opportunity for the Steadmores and former parishioner friends to press the flesh and exchange greetings.

It was a wonderful time. During the homily, Barclay challenged the worshippers to know whom they professed to be as baptised and confirmed members of the body of Christ. "What does it mean," he asked, "to be witnesses for Christ in a secular society?" He challenged them to live lives that would communicate to others that they were Christ's ambassadors in the community.

During the homily, Barclay looked down from the pulpit, directly at Harry and Annie who were sitting at the front in the second row of pews, and smiled as he uttered the phrase, "Wear your spiritual hats so that others will know that beneath that hat there lives a professing Christian."

Harry smiled back, for both knew that the wearing of hats was a metaphor that the two of them had employed many times in former days on the Harry Sting Show. Harry used to wear what Barclay labelled as a 'secular hat,' while Barclay, as Harry's guest was expected to spar with the host while wearing his 'spiritual hat.' The members in the pews, avid former listeners of the show, smiled as well. During the reception in the parish hall following the liturgy, many of the congregation grasped Barclay's hand and told him how that analogy of wearing hats resonated with them long after the show changed its format.

Barclay and Faith arrived at the Stings' residence mid-afternoon. Following a warm welcome, coffee, and hors d'oeuvres, Barclay begged off for a half hour snooze on the downstairs sofa in Harry's den as the morning service had been a bit stressful. Harry had ushered Barclay to his downstairs den and was inwardly thrilled that Barclay and he had become such close confidants that such a request could be so easily made. It was a compliment to their trust and openness with each other.

Barclay's short thirty-minute nap re-energized him and he joined Annie, Faith and Harry upstairs in the living room. The three were laughing as they recalled the various events that brought them together well over three years ago.

The dinner was a most pleasant occasion. Annie had prepared a crock pot meal consisting of beef, potatoes, onions, carrots, and golden mushroom soup. She had nixed the idea of going to the Red Pagoda, and decided on a simple meal where they could share their time around the dining room table. Following second helpings by both Barclay and Harry, the table was cleared and all four weighed into blueberry pie purchased from the local bake shop and coffee.

Harry and Barclay moved downstairs to Harry's study while Faith and Annie remained upstairs in the family room. It didn't take long for Harry to maneuver into a serious conversation with his old, trusted friend.

"Barclay, it's been a wonderful move for me, joining St. Bart's, taking on the directorship at the Samaritan Inn, and helping out the Diocese as Communications Director for the Bishop. But now that everything has fallen into place, I keep feeling that there must be another step in the process. I can't quite get my head around it all. It seems that I've reached a plateau in my life. We need to talk!"

There was a comfortable silence between the two. Finally, Barclay broke the lull of their conversation and asked, "What do you think is missing in your new roles as an involved Christian in the community?"

"Somehow," replied Harry, "I can't quite marry my position as the moderator on the Harry Sting Show and my other roles in the community. One should complement the other. But right now I seem to be wearing two hats, if you will. Remember how you used to pull that trick on me when you were a guest on the show? The 'secular hat' and the 'spiritual hat'? You would always say, 'Which one do you want me to wear today?'"

Barclay chuckled as he replied: "Quite a metaphor, isn't it? But let's talk some more. There is something beneath those hats that you haven't really fleshed out. What are some of the needs that you feel should be addressed in the town? What do you really want to address on your show? Let's first start with the Tangleville community."

"As a relatively new Christian I am puzzled that there exist so many different denominations in the town, indeed all around the world. Why in the world can't Christians get their act together instead of being so divided over their doctrine and witnessing to our 'anything goes' secular society. Think of how much more could be accomplished in the name of Christ if we could somehow all work together."

"Harry, I've wrestled with this all my life," his friend confided. "It is one of the major criticisms non-Christians love to throw up to us. Judaism is divided and Muslims are divided just as we are, but not to the same degree. Some estimate that there are more than thirty thousand variations of different Christian denominations in the world, with more being added daily. Perhaps the number is even greater. It is the greatest scandal in Christendom, a tragic distortion of our influence to others. If Christians can't openly agree with one another as to what Jesus taught, how in the world can we expect others to be His followers?"

"But, does it have to be so? Is there no hope of working together? Surely Christ never anticipated such division in his followers?"

"You have a twice weekly pulpit behind that microphone of yours. Why don't you explore solutions with your invited guests and listening call-in audience?"

"I've thought about trying something like that," said Harry. But for the life of me I can't seem to come up with a hook to introduce open discussion over the air. I want it to be introduced by someone other than myself so that I can appear to moderate suggestions which come up. Got any ideas how it can happen?"

"What have you got planned for tomorrow's show? What's the topic? Who is your guest?"

"I had a very influential guest booked now for some time. But this morning the office manager at AM KNOW called to tell me that she has had to send her regrets because she has to attend the funeral of a nephew in Petersville, just north of Kingsforth. She wants to be a guest as soon as possible in the future but has had to beg off tomorrow. As a result, I have no invited guest tomorrow for the show."

"All right. Here's a possible solution to a number of problems for you. Invite me to come as your guest for tomorrow's show. Explain over the air that your previously invited guest has had to cancel. Explain why. Then tell your audience that you have a surprise substitute: me! Then, after you give me some preliminary soft questions about what I am now doing following my retirement at St. Bart's, explain that I was a frequent guest on your past shows and inquire how I'm now occupying my time as a retired priest. I'll bring up a couple of issues that have been initiated by my ongoing research in contemporary concerns for the Church. I'll get around to opening up your misgivings and your questions about Christian denominational fracturing. Play along with me and let me be the instigator in setting the format for the day. In the second half of the show, the audience call-in section, challenge callers to respond to what I have said. You can go from there in up and coming shows."

"You're on! It sounds like old times together when you and I enjoyed a little rabble rousing together. Only this time, we will really be in sync with a higher purpose than just providing entertainment for the public."

"I have to be honest with you," said Barclay. "When I was on your show, I was always deadly serious in my stated convictions. I know that we at times seemed to be playing games, but never did I consider that I wasn't being true to my baptismal vows."

"I know, Barclay. Believe me, I know! Otherwise I would not have become a convert to the faith. But I bet that the listening audience will recall the sparks that used to fly when you were my guest."

Their conversation continued for the next hour as the flames in the wood-burning fireplace slowly turned to glowing embers. Harry and Barclay rejoined Faith and Annie in the upstairs den. The two were having an animated conversation over pictures in the Sting family photo albums, laughing together over the pictures of outdated clothing styles and hairdos.

"Do we look any older, Faith?" Annie was saying. "Let me put it another way. Do we have that many more wrinkles?"

"My eyesight is not what it used to be. But I'm not going there!" replied Faith. And they both laughed hysterically together.

Harry informed the two that Barclay was going to be his surprise guest on tomorrow's show. Annie wanted to know what the topic was going to be, but Harry, with a twinkle in his eye, simply replied, "Tune in and enjoy!"

After a few minutes of saying their goodnights, Barclay and Faith retired to the Stings' guest bedroom. It had been a long day and both were ready for a good night's rest. Following their individual prayers, Faith asked, "Bark, what's the show about tomorrow?"

"Oh, it's about Christians wearing so many different hats."

"I'll bet that Harry is planning a new project for Tangleville. Am I right?"

"Your intuitional abilities never cease to amaze me. Love ya! Goodnight!"

Barclay gave Faith a kiss and switched off the bedside light. It had been a most rewarding, yet unexpected day.

CHAPTER THREE

BARCLAY couldn't sleep! It was five o'clock Monday morning and he'd set the alarm in the Stings' guest room for six-thirty. At 6:25 a.m., he reached over and switched off the controls so that Faith would not be awoken, then put on the bathrobe which he unpacked from his suitcase and quietly crept downstairs to see if the Stings' automatic coffee maker was set for an early cup of coffee. It was.

Back in the bedroom, with the first cup of coffee at his right elbow, he finished his Bible readings and prayers, then reached for his Apple laptop. Faith was still sleeping soundly.

It was time to jot down a few of his thoughts - percolating in his mind since earlier that morning - to keep before him as he sat at the microphone on Harry Sting's 10:00 radio show. He found a few passages from the New Testament that he felt might be quoted on air, typed them out, and included them with his notes.

One such quotation kept going through his mind. It was an ancient question in the church. He didn't know who'd first formulated it, but it was as relevant today as in former times: the question, "If you were accused of being a Christian, would there be enough evidence to convict you?" He felt that somehow he had to initiate the opportunity to insert that quote on the show. It could be the focal point for him to further expand on the other concepts he knew that Harry wanted explored that morning.

Driving into the radio station parking lot brought back many memories of past times. He was thirty minutes early, and he wondered if any of the staff would remember him. Would Harry be there to greet him? Would he be as anxious as he used to be when he walked into the control room and waited for the On Air light to flash?

His thoughts were interrupted by the cheery voice of Cheryl Jones from behind the reception desk.

"Good morning Dr. Steadmore. Welcome home! We all missed you. Let me take your coat. Mr. Sting is already here and will join us in a minute of two."

She walked over to shake his hand, gave him a warm hug and retrieved his coat. "Now have a seat and let me get you a coffee. One cream, right?"

What a far cry it was from the time that Barclay had arrived for his first visit on Sting's show. Nobody welcomed him then! He was simply ushered into the control room and waited for Harry to show up, David before Goliath, so to speak.

Harry breezed into the room and grasped Barclay's hand.

"Great to have you here, Doctor. I'm so looking forward to today's show. Let's sit down for a few minutes and kind of run through where you want me to go today."

What a difference, thought Barclay. He wants to know where I want him to go! In former times, he would never tell me the topic for the day before the show was on the air. What a changed man Harry is!

They sat down at a small table next to the reception desk and Barclay gave Harry a few tips as to how he wanted to be interviewed and a couple of leading questions to ask.

"I've been working on what you said were your concerns during our time together last night," Barclay told him. "Why Christianity is so divided? Why all the denominational differences? I think I can work these misgivings of yours into the show. Let me set you up so that future guests can deal with these topics. We certainly can't deal with all your topics in one show!"

"Great! Let's go into the control room and get comfortable. Bring your coffee with you, Doctor. I'm so excited to get underway!"

The On Air light flashed and the engineer behind the glass that separated the control room from the broadcast area gave Harry the go signal.

"Good morning residents of Tangleville. This morning I have a very special guest before me: The Reverend Canon Doctor Barclay Steadmore, the former rector of downtown St. Bartholomew's Anglican Church. Doctor Steadmore, a good friend of mine, is no stranger to this show. It has been a couple of years or so since he was my guest here at AM KNOW. He and his spouse Faith retired and moved to that retirement town of Trinity Harbour. Doctor Steadmore was the guest preacher at St. Bart's yesterday and kindly agreed to stay over and be with us today. We are certainly privileged to have him with us. Good morning and welcome, Doctor Steadmore!"

"Thank-you Harry for that gracious welcome. Indeed, it's great to be back in Tangleville and to be with you today. How have you been? How is Annie, your vivacious wife?"

"We're both fine and very very busy. And you? What have you been up to during your retirement? Are you staying out of Faith's way? Fill us in how you're spending that spare time of yours."

"Well, I've been able to go about doing something that I've always wanted to do but never found the time to begin while I was rector at St. Bart's. I've been researching for a new book and am now about three quarters into the writing of it. Faith is so pleased that this has preoccupied much of my new-found freedom from ministry and has kept us from getting into each other's hair, as they say. She's very busy, as well, and sends you and Annie her greetings."

"I'm certain that my audience would like to hear more about your book. Give us a synopsis of what we can expect to read when it is published?" Harry asked him.

"It centers around one of the most perplexing scandals of Christianity which the secular world levels against the Church. The question is: why is the Christian world so divided in its doctrines? Why so many different denominations, each proclaiming the authentic teachings of Christ? New Christian denominations are being added to the list weekly. We Christians have, for centuries, been fighting amongst ourselves at the expense of not proclaiming the basic teachings of Christ to a needy world. That is the major problem I've set out to explore in my book. What can be done if we really are concerned about getting our acts together?"

"Why is it such a problem that Christianity is so divided?" Harry asked. "After all, aren't all Christian denominations teaching the message of Christ?"

Barclay replied, reading from his notes, "Critics are saying, 'If those Christians can't agree on what Christ taught, then how can they expect to make converts to the faith?' After all, Jesus prayed to his Father in

His High Priestly prayer, as we read in Saint John Chapter 17:21, 'I ask not only on behalf of these (his apostles), but also on behalf of those who will believe in me through their word, that they all may be one'. Today we're a long long way, as Christians, from being one in Christ."

"When did such divisions start in the church?"

"Very early! In fact, in the time of St. Paul himself. The twelve apostles had agreed to separate, to journey into the known world to preach the Good News of their resurrected Saviour. Without contact with these twelve eyewitnesses, living authorities who had walked, talked and travelled with Christ, differences soon began to emerge within the small church congregations as to what Christ had actually said and done. New leaders emerged, often with their own agendas and disputes emerged within the churches. The best record we have of this is in the First Letter of St. Paul to the Corinthian Church. They were divided over correct doctrine. St. Paul attempted to correct the matter and uttered those famous words applicable even to us today:

'From Saint Paul's First Letter to the Corinthians, Chapter 1, verse 10:

"Now I appeal to you brothers and sisters, by the name of our Lord Jesus Christ, that all of you should be in agreement and that there should be no divisions among you.'"

"Sounds like the same situation exists in our modern age," Harry noted. "You used the word 'authority'. Is the lack of agreed-upon authority the problem within Christianity?"

"Exactly, Harry! Each denomination, and in fact each individual believer, feels free to interpret the Holy Scriptures as they see fit, and in so doing become their own authorities in deciding what Christ taught. Individualism run amok! St. Paul, if he were with us today, would be horrified, aghast over where we find ourselves in our modern, secular times. Meanwhile, the world points its fingers at us and jeers: 'You're trying to convince us to become Christian when you can't even agree amongst yourselves as to what your founder taught? Get your act together first and then maybe you can be a credible voice in the competing pluralistic age.'"

"So, Dr. Steadmore, what is the answer? Is there a solution to the church's problem?"

"Certainly not immediately as we continue to dispute amongst ourselves. For centuries, we have focused on what divides us and have failed to celebrate what we have in common. It is up to us first to resolve our denominational differences. We will have to do it ourselves, if only we have the will to do so. Meanwhile, the scandal continues!"

The engineer from the other side of the glass partition separating the two rooms held up his hand signalling that a commercial break was coming. The On Air sign went out, and Harry and Barclay settled back into their chairs for the three-minute break. One of the office staff rushed in to refill their now empty coffee mugs.

Harry was smiling. "Great stuff, Doctor. But where are we going in the next fifteen minutes of the show? What do you want as a lead in for you to give some hope to the audience?"

"Let's give the folks a challenge, Harry! I'll suggest what might be a beginning step for Tangleville's Christians to consider to emerge a little closer together. You can then continue to explore further steps with future guests on upcoming shows. Let's challenge your listeners to suggest ways to begin to solve the problem. Let them be heard. I have a feeling that the desire and will are there to listen to those words of St. Paul, which he directed to this Christians at Corinth."

Radio stations are commercial enterprises and AM KNOW was no exception. The commercial being aired for the local hometown dealership, Tangleville Ford, was aimed at trying to convince folks that a new F150 was the best pickup on the market. During the commercial the enthusiastic salesman listed several ways in which the truck was different from its competitors. "So come in and check it out, Tangleville residents. There is nothing like it on the road today!"

Barclay looked over at Harry and grinned. "See Harry, it's everywhere. Sell the differences, not the similarities! But Christianity is not consumerism. True Christianity unites, not divides!"

Harry nodded just as the On Air signal flashed. There was no time for him to respond to Barclay's words.

"We're back, Tangleville! In case you missed the first segment of the show, our guest today is none other than the former rector of St. Bartholomew's who just articulated his frank conviction which may have disturbed some of you. He said that divided Christianity is one of the greatest scandals of modern times, holding the faith back from being a unified voice reaching out to future converts. Do you agree? I'll be waiting to hear what you have to say in the call-in section of the program. Now, back to our guest, Dr. Steadmore.

"Dr. Steadmore, I know you! I know that you are, at heart, an optimist. You have just given us a pretty pessimistic assessment on divided Christendom.

But I suppose that you are going to suggest a way out of this dilemma in which modern Christendom has evolved. Let's discuss how the churches, the many divided denominations, may begin to at least reverse the situation."

"I want to ask the listeners a question," Barclay said, "a question that has been around for centuries. How one may choose to answer the question will greatly influence the way we deal with one another. If you are ever accused of being a Christian, would there be enough evidence to convict you?"

"Where are you going with that, Doctor?"

"Well, it seems to me that to answer that question, one would have to be accused of putting into practice what Christ taught. By that I mean living out, demonstrating first principles of the Gospel. No judge or jury would be interested in the secondary variations of Christian doctrine developed over time, doctrinal fine points of theology debated by leading theologians. Splitting hairs, so to speak, the proper methods of baptism, clergy vestments, feast days: on and on it goes. Rather, the accused would have to answer to such questions as, 'Do you acknowledge Jesus Christ as God's Son? Do you attend public worship? Do you consider the Holy Scriptures as the revealed Word of God? Have you been baptised in the name of the Father, the Son, and the Holy Spirit? Do you confess Jesus Christ as Lord and Saviour?' See where I am going Harry? All Christians have the same answers to these questions! They share these in common."

"In other words, Doctor, you are stressing the basic similarities of Christianity and minimizing the differences in the practice of worship and the living out of the faith? Even though Christians may have different approaches to liturgy, they ought to be united in what really matters."

"That's it exactly, Harry. In his letter to the Romans St. Paul condemned their arguing over matters which divided the congregation and stressed mutual understanding. Adhering to first principles of the teachings of Christ, not what divides. I quote St. Paul in his Letter to the Romans, Chapter 14:13: 'Let us no longer pass judgment on one another, but resolve instead never to put a stumbling-block or hindrance in the way of another.'"

"It sounds to me, Doctor, that contemporary Christianity has failed to adhere to St. Paul's admonitions to the Church. We, in modern times are just as guilty of judging one another as they were back then."

"Absolutely!" Barclay agreed. "Now the question is, can we afford to continue as separated followers of Christ, disputing over our doctrinal differences, when the secular world writes us off as just another fragmented option amongst the world's other competing religions? Christianity no longer can afford to tolerate what divides us. For, as we now exist, we are a source of amusement and ridicule for non-believers."

"Time is almost up for today's program, Doctor. Let me know when your book has been published and I will announce it to my listeners. Thank-you for coming today. Any final words to add in the final ten seconds?"

This put Barclay on the spot, but he summed up by saying, "Let mutual love continue. Love never divides, but unites!"

The On Air sign went out and both leaned forward, shook hands, and smiled across the desk. They knew that it had been a great show. Harry and Barclay emerged from their chairs and walked together to the reception room. The goodbyes were quick, as Harry's next segment of the show, the call-in portion was due to begin in exactly ten minutes. Barclay and Harry hugged, told each other to bring greetings to their spouses, and departed.

It was a short drive to the Stings' residence where Barclay knew that Faith would be packed and ready to begin the journey back to

Trinity Harbour. It was a warm sunny day and Barclay dropped the top of their convertible Mustang He phoned ahead and by the time he arrived, their luggage was waiting on the front steps, the front door slightly ajar. Annie and Faith were laughing inside. Harry loaded their bags into the trunk of the car, pushed open the front door and interrupted the conversation of the two amused best friends.

"What's so funny?" he inquired.

"Oh, we're just trying to find a practical way of resolving your plea for simplifying our two different Christian liturgical ways of worshipping God. How in the world can a Russian Orthodox service and the Anglican liturgy ever find commonality?"

"Maybe if Anglicans learned to speak Russian," Barclay quipped. As he said it he thought to himself, "It's so easy to talk about Christian unity, but to achieve it will require the wisdom of Solomon and the self-sacrifices of the ancient martyrs."

CHAPTER FOUR

HARRY was in his office bright and early the next morning. The second half of the previous day's program, the call-in section, had been one of the most spirited thirty minutes he'd had in recent weeks. The audience was split over Steadmore's claim that it was a scandal that Christendom was divided, labelled a fractured world religion in the minds of non-believers. Some callers tried to justify the existence of many denominations, each one proclaiming to convey true Christianity. Others were challenged by Steadmore's plea for stressing that which major denominations share in common, and thus minimizing doctrinal differences. It was evident to Harry that Steadmore's thesis for unity was entirely missed. Now Harry was faced with the challenge of where to go on future shows. Perhaps it might be wise to invite clergy from the major denominations of Tangleville to be guests on his show. This, he reasoned, would give credence to what Steadmore had said, or would give validation to those call-in people who were opposed to any kind of fellowship with members of other denominations.

He decided to call the Reverend Doctor Angus McLaughlin at St. Andrew's Presbyterian Church in downtown Tangleville and invite him for lunch at the Samaritan Inn. Doctor McLaughlin readily accepted and agreed to a Thursday luncheon.

* * *

Tuesday and Wednesday were stressful days for Harry. The battered young woman who had arrived at the reception desk last week, accompanied by a female police officer, was not doing well. She had been admitted to the Tangleville hospital for observation and the medical staff was concerned that she may have received a concussion as a result of her live-in partner's drunken attack. After a two-day stay for assessment, she was released and returned to the care of the Samaritan Inn.

Now the staff was involved with piles of paper work. She needed counselling, sound assistance, and legal advice from a lawyer assigned to investigate the incident. She was advised to press charges against her violent live-in, who meanwhile had been confined to a cell at the local downtown police precinct. The woman refused, and Harry and Harriet the on-staff social worker were wrestling with the best way to ensure that the woman could be helped to re-enter living on her own. Harriet and Harry agreed that a four-week residency at the Samaritan Inn domestic violence shelter was the best option to pursue. Both stressed the importance for the victim to press charges with police. In the meantime, the police had no option but to release the violent offender.

Harry needed a change of venue, and he was so looking forward to Doctor McLaughlin's visit for lunch and conversation at noon today. The two had met only briefly before. Doctor McLaughlin was the long-time minister at St. Andrew's and was highly respected in town. For years he had authored a weekly column in the Tangleville Mirror, the widely-read newspaper which sixty-nine percent of the town's residents had delivered to their door.

Harry wanted to accomplish two objectives during the luncheon. He needed to find out if the highly influential clergyperson was on side, in agreement with the statements Steadmore had delivered on Monday's show. More importantly, would the brilliant pulpit orator and erudite word craftsman be interested in taking the lead in pursuing steps to address Steadmore's accusations of Christian disunity? Harry knew that he needed co-operation and leadership from local clergy to address Steadmore's challenge. He himself could be behind the scenes as a cheerleader, but if transformation was to take place it must originate with religious leaders, who in turn could challenge their congregations to become change agents for renewal.

Doctor McLaughlin arrived three minutes to noon and reported in at the reception desk. He was wearing his clerical collar and was immediately recognized by the manager Jean who had been forewarned that Harry was expecting a clergy guest. Before Doctor McLaughlin could identify himself, Jean walked around the counter, extended her hand to meet the expected guest and greeted him with a warm smile.

"Good morning Doctor McLaughlin. Welcome to the Samaritan Inn. Mr. Sting is expecting you. Please follow me and I'll show you the way to his office."

Angus nodded to himself, seemingly impressed. The hallways were wide, well lighted and the floors sparkled under the wax on the newly polished tiles. Harry's office was halfway down the hall to the right, his office door open.

"Mr. Sting, Doctor McLaughlin has arrived. Doctor McLaughlin, Mr. Sting!"

Harry sprang from his office chair and rushed to greet his guest. "Thank-you Jean, but we've met once before. I believe it was at a town council meeting, wasn't it Doctor McLaughlin?"

"Please call me Angus! Yes, we were both there, if I rightly recall, because we were objecting to the timing of the Santa Claus parade which Tangleville had announced was going to begin at ten o'clock on a Sunday morning. We both made presentations to council and persuaded councillors to change the time to take place the same day, but in the afternoon. Remember? We argued that the morning time would interfere with Sunday services of worship. And we won!"

"Welcome Angus! Yes, I remember," Harry replied. "We went out afterwards to the local coffee shop for coffee and apple critters. . We pulled off quite a coup, didn't we? I believe that that's the last time we have spoken."

Harry directed him to one of the comfortable leather chairs in front of his desk and sat down in the one beside it. It would be obvious to Angus that Harry was not sitting behind his desk, but sitting beside him demonstrating that the visit was one to put his guest at ease.

"You know, Angus, I still can't quite understand why the town council granted us that request. They didn't need to do so. How do you explain it?"

There was a twinkle in the Reverend's eye. "I think that if they didn't, they believed that I would write up the denial in my weekly newspaper column and it would give them a hard time come next election. Christians don't easily forget such things! We are taken for granted in so many ways nowadays. Secularism rules, doesn't it?"

That was exactly what Harry needed to hear, and he knew he may have found an ally in Doctor McLaughlin.

After a few more minutes of small talk, Harry arose, walked to the office door, leading his guest as he went. "Let's go down to the cafeteria, Angus. I have a table for two set aside for us. I'm not sure what the menu is today, but there will be enough variety that I'm certain that it will tide us over to dinner time."

The two sat down across from one another and perused the menu for the day: vegetable or cream of celery soup, hot beef sandwiches and rice, or liver and onions for the main course, ice cream or tapioca pudding, tea or coffee.

The lady on serving duty, one of the guests enrolled at the Samaritan Inn domestic violence shelter, was serving her time as a volunteer. All residents were required to do voluntary tasks while in house at the Inn.

"What will it be, Angus?" Harry asked.

"Let's go for the celery soup and the hot beef sandwich. Easy on the gravy, please."

The lady took his order and then turned to Harry. "Your usual, Mr. Sting? I know that whenever liver and onions are served that you never choose anything else."

"You bet, and I'll have the vegetable soup as well."

She hurried off to place their orders and Harry felt that it was time to begin to address the real reason that Doctor McLaughlin was his invited guest.

"Angus, did you listen to the broadcast last Monday with my guest Dr. Steadmore?"

"I sure did! It was quite a show. I've been thinking about what was said for the last few days."

Harry was almost holding his breath in anticipation of Angus' assessment of the event. "Tell me, what did you hear Doctor Steadmore say?"

"What really impressed me was his plea, his call for Christians to accentuate that which they share in common, and minimise their liturgical differences. I particularly agreed with his assessment that secular society writes off Christianity as such a divided faith that our message is not to be taken seriously nor even considered when secular events collide with church functions, not to mention moral positions which are not favoured by Christians. I almost applauded out loud when he called it so accurately in our secular age."

"That's what I heard too, Angus. And I'm determined that things have to change. We denominational Christians are much much closer to each other than the world gives us credit. Just think what a force for change we could be if we agreed to work together."

The main course had arrived at their table and Harry asked Doctor McLaughlin to bless the food. They bowed their heads as Angus prayed and after the 'Amen' was pronounced Harry crossed himself.

"You must be an Anglican," Angus grinned as he observed the subtle making of the cross.

"Yes, the secret is out. Doctor Steadmore and I are great friends. That's why he was on my show. But tell me: any idea how we may go about getting Steadmore's criticism of modern Christianity addressed?" Harry made certain that he stressed the 'we' in this question.

"Well," Angus replied, "there's no way that the two of us can do it by ourselves. If anything is about to change, it is going to require the combined co-operation of as many denominational leaders as possible. We will have to make it clear that such an alliance of Christians will stress what we hold in common, and that in no way are we advocating changing or altering our individual liturgical practices. It may be too much to hope for, but unity of purpose might trump the differences in our individual denominations' worship styles over centuries of divergences. I can't imagine our Lord sending out His twelve apostles expecting them to preach about their individual hobby horses."

This was exactly what Harry wanted to hear. They continued their discussion, both choosing the tapioca pudding for dessert. Over coffee, they seemed to be exactly on the same page. Harry finally asked, "Can we meet again soon, to take it to the next step, Angus?"

"Tell you what, Harry. I've got a meeting with Father Leo Mahoney next Tuesday. You may know him, he's the Roman Catholic priest over at St. Anne's Parish. Let me run over some of our concerns with him. I'm betting that we may find an ally in him. He's got a big parish and I know that he is concerned about the Church losing influence in the world."

"I love it, Angus. And perhaps you might get in touch with Canon Hudson over at St. Bart's. I think the three of you would make a powerful trinity of voices, modern day versions of Matthew, Mark, Luke, and John."

"That would mean another addition to the group, Harry. Who do you suggest?

"Well there are Lutherans, and Baptists, Pentecostals, and Orthodox clergy in town to start with. Take your pick!"

"Are you sure that you are not suggesting the choosing of twelve members, Harry?" That's the number our Lord chose, remember?"

It was a very satisfied Harry who walked Doctor McLaughlin to his car out in the parking lot. God certainly does work in amazing ways, he thought to himself as he returned to his office to face the day's challenge.

Chapter Five

DR. McLaughlin's head was spinning with ideas. It had been some time since he had been so excited about a new challenge for himself and the possibility of the Christian Church challenging complacent and jaded secular society. He could hardly wait to meet with Father Mahoney over at St. Anne's. He wrestled with Harry's suggestion that he ought to call Canon Hudson at St. Bartholomew's parish.

The more he thought about it, the more he became convinced it would be beneficial to do so prior to his meeting with Father Leo. If Canon Hudson could be persuaded to come on board, then he would be able to advise Father Leo that it wasn't just his own congregation that was in favour of action. Angus knew that he hadn't yet taken the challenge to his own people at St. Andrew's, but he knew his people. After all, he had been their minister for many years and he knew that if he handled the challenge well, they would be persuaded to co-operate. They were always searching for ways to become more active in the Tangleville community.

When Angus arrived at his office, he picked up his telephone, and dialed up St. Bart's. Hannah answered in her usual professional and welcoming voice, "St. Bartholomew's Anglican Parish. Hannah Fisher speaking. How may I help you?"

"Good afternoon Hannah. This is Angus McLaughlin calling. I am the minister over at St. Andrew's down the street. I don't think we've met!"

"No, we haven't Doctor, but I have had the opportunity of learning a little about you from your receptionist, Heather MacDonald. She is my next door neighbor and we often share stories over tea about our two congregations and our similar church duties. How may I help you today?"

"Is Canon Hudson in? Do you think that he might have the time to speak with me?"

"Yes, he's in. I'm sure that he will be happy to. Let me check for you. Please hold."

Hannah put Doctor McLaughlin on hold and stuck her head through the door to the office of Canon Hudson.

"Canon, Doctor McLaughlin from St. Andrew's down the street is on the line and wishes to talk with you. Shall I put him through?"

"By all means, Hannah. I've been wanting to meet him ever since I took over for Doctor Steadmore."

Hannah connected the two clergymen and hung up her phone to continue working on the bulletin for the coming Sunday.

"Good afternoon, Doctor," said Hudson. "It's about time that we actually speak. I'm afraid that I'm amiss in not taking you out for lunch."

"Good afternoon Canon Hudson. I too have been at fault. After all, we only exist a few blocks apart from one another. It's time that we meet in person!"

"Call me Matthew, Doctor. I don't like such formal titles between fellow workers in the kingdom."

"That goes for me also, Matthew. I'm Angus! Say, do you have a few minutes to spare this afternoon? I'd like to drop in to discuss a matter with which I think you may be able to help out. I need your opinion as a brother Christian leader in town. I promise not to take up too much of your time."

"Let's see, it is now two-thirty. I've got no appointments after three today. I'm trying to renew our contract for maintenance on our photocopier for the coming year. Will three fifteen or soon after work for you?"

"That's just fine with me. I'll bring coffee. What do you drink?"

"A small dark roast with one cream, Angus. See you then."

Well that went just dandy, Angus thought to himself. Now if only Hudson can see fit to come aboard. Dark roast and cream to the rescue!

Angus could hardly wait to meet with Canon Hudson. "How would he broach the topic of working together with an Anglican priest? Over the centuries there had been such a rivalry between Presbyterians and Anglicans. History is history," he thought to himself. But history is in the making every day. Times have changed and it is about time to rewrite the times.

Angus entered the drive-thru at the new downtown coffee shop The Sir Java Supreme, ordered two regular coffees, small, and one dark roast, cream and sugar on the side. Perhaps Hannah may still be at her desk, and he wanted to make sure that she wasn't left out in his visit to St. Bart's.

He parked his Honda Accord in one of the empty spaces in the large parking lot, locked the car doors, and walked toward the front entrance of the parish office. Before he could reach for the handle, the door opened. Before him stood a smartly dressed middle-aged woman.

"I saw you parking outside," she said. "I'm Hannah. Welcome!"

Angus was glad that he had three coffees in tow. Hannah certainly was endearing herself to him. So far, so good!

After a few brief minutes of conversation, her coffee in hand, Hannah ushered Angus into Canon Hudson's office. There were a few moments of introductions and Matthew and Angus sat down across from one another around a small table in the rector's well-furnished inner office.

The two shared information about their families, their callings to ordained ministry, church challenges and concerns in the community and finally Angus felt it was the perfect opportunity to introduce the real reason for his visit.

"Did you hear Doctor Steadmore's portion of the Harry Sting Show last Monday?"

"I sure did," replied Matthew. "I don't know if you are aware that he preached here at St. Bart's the Sunday before the show. After the Sunday liturgy, Harry and Annie, Barclay and Faith, my spouse Margaret, better known to most as Maggie, and I shared lunch together at the Surf 'n Turf. We discussed his Sunday sermon and Harry indicated how he wished there was some way the sermon topic could be shared with his listening audience. I guess that they must have come to an agreement to do so, because Barclay was Harry's guest on the show the next morning."

"What did you think of his plea for Christian denominational co-operation in this secular age in which we now live?"

"If only it could be possible!" responded Matthew. "I know that we as clergy may be in favor, but I'm not so certain that some of the life-long traditionalists in the pews would come around to seeing it necessary, even beneficial, to work together with the other 'so-called Christians,' as they might put it. We'd really have to do our homework in convincing people that the need is there to bridge our perceived different denominational traditions."

"Do you think the need is there, Matthew? Was Dr. Steadmore an alarmist? You know him much better than I do!"

"No! No! He was dead on in his accusation about scandal within Christianity. His suggestion of accentuating what we share in common and minimizing our doctrinal differences is precisely what the secular world needs to hear. A divided voice in Christianity is easy to dismiss, even to ridicule. But, if we could only become a major, unified voice in the affairs of this town, we would have to be taken seriously."

"But, what about our different styles of worship, our various liturgical approaches to Sunday services? How do we explain those to the complacent, non-religious masses?"

"That's where we don't need to change, Angus! Secular society doesn't have a clue nor care about such practices. It simply thinks that we are so divided that we have nothing at all in common. Thus, we are not taken seriously since we have no organized voice. But you and I both know that all Christians share far more in common than that which divides us!"

"I'm delighted to hear you say this," Angus said. "Would you be willing to work with me to explore how we might address Steadmore's concern? I've met with Harry Sting and he's more than on board in giving us the air time at AM KNOW. I'm going to visit Father Leo over at St. Anne's next Tuesday and invite his participation as well. Can you imagine how powerful a voice the three of us could be in Tangleville if we joined forces? Why the public wouldn't know how to respond to the Anglicans, Presbyterians and Roman Catholics – three amigos! Sting would have a field day if all three of us were to appear together on one of his shows. Talk about a public pulpit for us!"

"I'm in, Angus! Tell Father Leo that he can count on me if he is willing to come aboard. I can hardly wait to hear what he will say to you!"

Angus stood up and grasped Matthew's hand within both of his. His smile reached from ear to ear as he thanked his Anglican clerical neighbor for his intention to explore that which he was convinced was a radical, timely opportunity for Christians to be an audible and visible force in Tangleville. The two promised to pray for each other, their congregations and to ask God's blessing upon their proposed plans.

Chapter Six

AS Harry drove to his office, his mind was anywhere but on his driving. He almost ran a red light at the intersection of Maple and Elm Streets as he rehearsed in his mind the topics to be addressed at the upcoming Board of Directors' meeting. The main items for the event were standard ones: the approval of the agenda for the evening, minutes of the last monthly meeting, the treasurer's report, ongoing maintenance concerns, the social worker's report and, of course, his own

He was well aware that the main issue of the meeting was going to center on fundraising for the coming year. The Board had previously approved the motion for an ambitious building program to expand the number of beds at the Inn. They had not yet addressed how the funds would be raised to pay for such a major undertaking. This, Harry knew, was going to incite plenty of conflicting opinions as to which methods of doing so were in the best interest of the charitable institution. As an official non-religious institution, would the Inn be willing to receive donations from any and all donors? The organization had received its charitable status a few months ago and was now able to issue tax receipts to those who were willing to donate.

Would Harry's morals get in the way now that he was a practising Christian in his day-to-day life? What if the local strip club in downtown Tangleville decided to donate and wished to have its name published amongst the list of donors? What if the downtown casino was willing to make a large contribution on the condition its donation received widely publicized notice in the Samaritan Inn newsletter? The local brewery would certainly be willing to financially contribute, but since many of the Inn's residents were in house because of alcoholic spousal abuse, would it be wise to accept the brewery's funds?

Harry knew that the Board members would be all over the map when it came to dealing with such decisions. Could he wear two hats, his secular one and his sacred one as he chaired the meeting? The proverbial question would certainly rear its head: Does the end justify the means?

Harry was well aware of the distinction between two main ethical positions in order to answer such a question: deontology and consequentialism. He wondered if he should explain the differences to the board members when they meet. He knew that Deontology argues that whether an action is 'good' or 'bad' depends on some quality of the action itself. This argument insists that certain actions are inherently bad, such as murder, torture, stealing, lying, even water boarding. Immanuel Kant had insisted that such actions are never to be considered justifiable.

Consequentialism takes a different view and argues that whether an action is 'good' or 'bad' depends upon the outcome of the action. The best course of action is one that maximizes utility. So the end does justify the means in some cases. The 'white lie' is not a 'black lie' they often argue.

Harry could take some comfort in knowing that a Salvation Army officer, Major James Huff, was a member of the Board of Directors of the charitable organization. Perhaps he would be able to help the board work through such questions of accepting donations from certain secular groups. After all, William Booth, the founder of the Salvation Army was often criticized over accepting tainted money from wealthy donors. Major Huff would certainly be able to explain Booth's position as he had allegedly said, "We will wash it with tears of the widows and the orphans and lay it on the altar of humanity." What he meant was, accept the gift, pray for the giver and use the money for the good of the needy.

Isn't it interesting? thought Harry, how a Christian is faced at times to make decisions that are not clearly permitted or denied in Holy Scripture. To be human is to be accountable to God and to reason at the same time!

Harry's thoughts were interrupted by the buzzing of his office intercom.

"Mr. Sting," Jean said, "Bishop Strictman from the Diocesan Office is on the line. He says that it's urgent."

"Put him through, Jean. I haven't heard from him for a few weeks."

Jean was the one person who was indispensable to the Samaritan Inn organization. Forty-three years of age, she had worked for the Inn from its beginning. A mother of two teenaged children, abandoned by her husband shortly after the birth of her second child, she'd had to go it alone. She applied for the position of manager and excelled in the role, while taking night courses at the university to earn her business degree. Harry leaned on her time and time again for her help in the day to day running of the organization. Each year Harry insisted on a pay raise for her, knowing that if she decided to move to another position in the town, with a bigger salary, that she could never be replaced.

Harry picked up the phone.

"Good morning, Bishop Strictman. Great to hear your voice!"

"Harry, I'm afraid that I bear some unfortunate news. As Communications Director for the Diocese, I will require your help, I'm afraid. Can you drop everything and rush over to my office to meet with me and our lawyers for a four o'clock meeting? I'll explain what it is all about when we meet."

The Diocesan offices were a good forty five-minute drive for Harry. He could sense the urgency in the Bishop's voice and wondered, what will it be this time? He knew that the media must be about to investigate something that would not reflect positively for the Diocese. As the Communications Director, the Bishop would likely be calling upon him once again to speak to the press. It was not an easy task to be on the other side of the microphone.

Harry arrived five minutes early for the meeting. Mary Baldwin, the office administrator, greeted him and ushered him into Bishop Strictman's inner office. The Chancellor, himself a lawyer, and his partner in the law firm were already present. They were seated around the long oak desk in the working area of the room and all rose to greet Harry. They quickly shook hands and Bishop Strictman began the meeting with the words, "Thank-you for coming on such short notice, gentlemen. We've got a serious problem to handle! Mary, as usual, take careful notes for us, please. Of course, people, everything said here today is strictly confidential."

The Bishop methodically outlined the details of an accusation that could be about to make news involving a small country parish, St.

Hilda's-in-the-Field, at the extreme north edge of the Diocese. The Reverend Joseph Clayborne, rector of the parish was being accused of stealing money from the parish rector's discretionary fund. Jim and Judy Sallow, a parish husband and wife couple who served as treasurer for the parish, had contacted Bishop Strictman and accused Father Clayborne of theft.

"What is the evidence of such a charge?" the Chancellor, James Hunter, asked.

"Well, it seems that Father Clayborne for the last three months has been asking for double his parish allotment for his discretionary fund," replied Bishop Strictman.

"What's wrong with that?" insisted Hunter. "Clayborne is not required to divulge to anyone how that money is spent. It is strictly up to him as he sees needs in the parish community. What evidence do the Sallows have that Clayborne misappropriated funds?"

"Well, it seems that Father Joseph has been observed driving a new Subaru Forester SUV, and the Sallows don't think that he can afford such a vehicle on the salary the parish is paying. They claim that he must be using church funds entrusted to him to make payments on the new set of wheels."

"That would never hold up in court," sniffed Hunter. "It's merely speculation at this point! There has got to be more behind the story than that! Has there been bad blood, so to speak, between the rector and the Sallows?"

"There has," replied Bishop Strictman. "They have complained to me, in written form, twice before, that they do not approve of Father Joseph's worship style. He is too 'high church' for their taste. They want a more 'free-wheeling' style of liturgy, more akin to the thriving non-denominational congregation a kilometre or so down the road from St. Hilda's-in-the Field."

"So Father Joseph won't budge then?" suggested David McKnight, Hunter's partner in the law firm. "Have the Sallows indicated how soon they may go public with their accusation?"

"They gave me a week to publically dismiss Father Clayborne. If I don't they will go to The Mirror and then to the local television station. I have to be frank with you right now. I'm not about to lift Father Joseph's licence at this juncture. But I need your advice as to how to deal with both parties in a fair and just manner."

Harry, up to this point, had not contributed to the discussion. He realized that his role was one that would have to deal with the media if the story were to break. He respected the Bishop's authority and knew him to be a fair and wise individual. Nevertheless, he felt obligated to ask the Bishop what seemed to him to be a logical question.

"Bishop, we've spent considerable time addressing the Sallows. What does Father Joseph have to say about all of this?"

"Fair question, Harry! He's out of town at the moment, but I've sent him an email asking him to meet with me tomorrow as soon as he is back to his parish. He has agreed to do so."

Hunter, not a man to waste time, suggested that after the Bishop met with Father Clayborne that he set a time to re-convene. It was paramount, he insisted, that they meet before the deadline that the Sallows had arbitrarily set.

The four agreed, and Mary Baldwin was instructed to email the minutes of the meeting to each of the three invited participants. In the interim, Bishop Strictman was advised to contact the Sallows and to impress upon them that they were not to be in touch with any media.

On the way back to Tangleville Harry's mind was racing. Another hat to wear in the community, he concluded. What if the Sallows' accusations were true? What if they weren't? Being a long time media junkie, somehow he was certain that the story was bound to have legs and he would be right in the middle to be called to address the fallout to the secular public. How ironic, he thought to himself. Once upon a time on my radio show I thrived on this kind of controversy.

Now he was on the other side of the microphone, a Christian who was obligated to make certain that whatever he said to the public on behalf of the Diocese, was reasonable and balanced.

CHAPTER SEVEN

ANGUS had not formally met Father Leo Mahoney over at St. Anne's parish, but they had nodded briefly to one another during a Tangleville Council meeting a year ago. Both were in attendance at the meeting to voice their opposition to the Town Council's agenda motion to prohibit Christmas crèches on public lands in the community. The motion was passed, but did not restrict churches from doing so on parish properties. It was another win, Angus had concluded, in favor of political correctness: the secular voice of pluralism!

St. Anne's was a rather imposing structure on the corner of Maple and Iris Streets. The parish was well over one hundred and fifty years old, a plum appointment for the last thirty years for senior priests in the Roman Catholic Diocese. For Father Leo to be the senior priest in the parish, he must carry considerable respect with his Bishop, thought Angus. He must be a person who carries weight in his diocese.

Angus arrived with five minutes to spare before his ten o'clock appointment. He was warmly welcomed upon arrival by the parish receptionist, Karen O'Toole and Mary O'Brien the office administrator. They took his coat and invited him to be seated in one of the large leather covered chairs in the waiting room of the well-furnished reception area.

"Father Leo is on the phone at the moment, Dr. McLaughlin. Would you like a coffee or tea as you wait for him to receive you?" the receptionist asked.

"No thanks," replied Angus. "I'm just fine! I'll wait for Father Leo. This leather chair is so comfortable, I'm not sure that I want to get out of it!"

He smiled, trying to put the receptionist at ease. After all, he was sure that it wasn't every day that a Presbyterian cleric was received as a guest in a Roman Catholic administrative office.

Father Leo soon rushed over to meet Angus. He was an imposing man, immaculately attired in a well-tailored black suit and a black clerical shirt with a crisp white Roman collar.

"Good morning Doctor McLaughlin. Welcome to St. Anne's. I'm Leo Mahoney!"

As he greeted Angus, he warmly embraced him in a firm bear hug and pointed towards his large, tastefully furnished office. They sat down together in large leather chairs facing one another. It was obvious to Angus that Father Leo was treating him with acceptance and respect as a fellow cleric in the community.

"Father, thank-you for seeing me today. And please drop the 'Doctor' and just call me Angus!"

"And I'm simply Leo! The 'Father' title isn't necessary when two brothers in Christ are speaking in private. Again, welcome!"

What a welcoming invitation that was, thought Angus. There were times not too long ago when Christian clerics of different denominations, then considered theological enemies, would not greet one another as brothers in Christ. Times have certainly changed for the better!

Angus and Leo spent the first fifteen minutes of their time together getting to know each other: where they grew up as children, where they attended university, and how they ended up as ordained clergy. Both had entered seminary right after graduation from their undergraduate degree, Angus with a major in history and Leo in philosophy. Both expressed how ministry involved the best of times and times of sheer endurance. They laughed at how similar their roles really were in Tangleville - indeed in any parish in which they may find themselves serving. It was obvious to Angus that they both shared much more in common than that which separated their two denominations. Angus was convinced that now was the right time to reveal to Leo the real purpose of his visit.

"Leo," he began. "I'm here to discuss with you a concern that has been taking up a great deal of my time lately. I'm convinced that we Christians in this secular society in which we now live, are increasingly becoming a voice that is ignored, ridiculed and destined to be silenced. I don't think that we as people of faith are taken seriously in this ever-increasing anti-religious era. The popular view of those outside the Christian Churches is that we are so divided that we no longer present a challenge to society's so called progressive changes. Does any of this resonate with you?"

Father Leo grinned and leaned toward him. "Do you remember the first time you and I actually were in the same room together? We didn't get to shake hands, but it was when we made separate presentations to Tangleville Town Council objecting to their agenda item to prevent the placement of Christian crèches on public property. We lost the challenge. We might have done far better if we had made a joint presentation instead of two separate ones. Yes! I hear you, Angus. We learned a valuable lesson that evening, didn't we?"

"Let me be perfectly up front with you," Angus told his colleague. "I've already spoken with Canon Hudson over at St. Batholomew's Anglican Parish, and he and I are convinced it's time for Christians to get their act together when it comes to informing those outside Christianity that we share far more in common than that which separates us. I told Canon Hudson that I was going to meet with you today. We are hopeful - indeed optimistic - that you may be sharing our concerns, and, Leo, here it comes: we're convinced that if we three clergy agree to work together as a trio, we may be able to initiate a movement that reverses the decline of the voice of Christendom here in the town. Canon Hudson will work with me if you are willing also to do so. How does all this strike you?"

"You are aware, I'm certain, of how our new Pope Francis has opened the door for ecumenical Christian dialogue," Leo said. "I've been waiting for years for such a Vatican directive. My Bishop is pre-disposed to see the Holy Father's request become a reality. Yes! Yes indeed! I'm only too willing to work with you and Canon Hudson. When do you propose we begin to hold our meetings?"

"Leo, your response and commitment are an answer to prayer! Canon Hudson and I are not at all interested in our three denomina-tions developing a common liturgy. That is not our aim. We simply want to put together a document that celebrates what we share as Christians, not what divides us! I'm convinced that the secular world will be very surprized to learn that we hold so much in common! Will it work for you if we meet twice a month?

"I'm OK with that. Let's begin to hold our meetings on each other's church premises," Leo suggested. "It will soon be noticed that three neighboring clerics are meeting on a regular basis. Why, people may begin to suspect that something out of the ordinary is taking place.

Rumors will spread, and that may be exactly what's needed to launch our proposed stratagem."

"Twice a month meetings should be fine if we can agree on which day of the week it will be. Some of us take Friday off, some Mondays. What is your practice, Angus?"

"I usually try to take Mondays. I don't know about Canon Hudson. Let me get in touch with him and get back to you. What would you say if we aim for luncheon meetings where the host church provides a simple lunch ... perhaps sandwiches and soup ... you know what I mean?"

Angus was on cloud nine. He could hardly wait for the first working luncheon session for the three leaders to begin putting their heads together to let the people of Tangleville know that Christians may be an up and coming united voice in the community.

Now to let Harry Sting know that the three amigos had saddled up and were riding into town!

CHAPTER EIGHT

HARRY'S desk clock flashed 10:26 as he sat in the big leather chair in his office. Doctor McLaughlin had called a week before informing him that his meetings with Canon Hudson and Father Mahoney had been extremely positive. The three clerics were going to meet on Wednesdays, twice a month, starting a week from today.

What was of a major concern for Harry was finally diffused by the outcome of the Board of Directors 'meeting at the Samaritan Inn which took place last week. It was a long, drawn-out event with heated debate over fundraising for the expansion of the premises.

Harry was relieved that the means of fundraising for the expansion had finally hammered out a conclusion that he was able to live with. The expansion of the facility already approved at a previous meeting was not the issue. How the funds were to be raised was the sticky point. There was no way that he was willing to accept donations from groups and businesses that he felt were objectionable enterprises, and then to include the names of such donors in the annual list of supporters available to the general public.

The Board was divided over this issue, some insisting that any and all donations, regardless of how the monies had been gained, should be freely accepted and acknowledged. Others felt that the Board ought not to be used as an advertisement for the advancement of those who wish to legitimatize their existence. At length, after almost an hour of open and frank discussion, a compromise was suggested that Harry was able to accept.

Thanks to Major John Huff's proposal, they finally agreed to accept all monies donated, no questions asked as to the source of how the funds were gained, but the Samaritan Inn would no longer publish the names of the donors. If donations were made, Major Huff argued, they would be done so in the true spirit of benevolence.

Harry was so relieved by this motion. He took Major Huff aside after the meeting and personally thanked him for such a wise and astute proposal. Major Huff smiled and said, "The Salvation Army has a long history of dealing with 'filthy lucre' and making it acceptable in God's service!" Harry understood exactly what Major John meant.

Mary Baldwin, the Diocesan Administrator, had sent an email to Harry, James Hunter, and David McKnight yesterday, requesting their presence for a Thursday three o'clock gathering at the Synod Office. Harry assumed that the Bishop must have had a meeting with Father Clayborne, and was going to pursue the matter of the Sallows' accusations of Clayborne's absconding with church funds.

It was a bright sunny day, and Harry looked forward to the drive in the Audi Annie had given to him as a forty-sixth birthday present. It was difficult for Harry to keep the German luxury sedan under the posted freeway speed limit, and there were times when he didn't succeed. This morning was one of them, and so he arrived at the Synod Office fifteen minutes early.

Mary and Harry spent the waiting time together discussing her new Camaro convertible which was parked out in the parking lot. Harry, up to then, was not aware that she was a 'car guy,' and was almost disappointed to end their conversation when James and David arrived, and together they were ushered into Bishop Strictman's office.

"Welcome friends! Thank you for coming today on such short notice. I think that you are going to be surprised by what I am going to reveal to you. I had a rather unexpected explanation from Father Clayborne," grinned Bishop Strictman.

The four of them were seated around the large oak table in the Bishop's inner office. Bishop Strictman leaned forward in his chair and with a detectable smile on his face, began:

"What I'm going to tell you is strictly confidential. Not a word of this is to go from this room. I had to promise Father Clayborne that I would not reveal a word of what he revealed to me this past week, except to you three. So you are bound to secrecy!

Father Clayborne admitted to repeatedly asking for additional funds for his rector's discretionary fund for a reason that really warmed my heart. The Sallows have a married daughter living with her husband and a new infant daughter in the next town over from the Sallows' home. The baby's father, the Sallows' son-in-law, married their daughter against their wishes and following the marriage, they have never spoken to their new in-law, nor met their granddaughter. They disowned the three completely.

Now Father Clayborne was contacted by the daughter and son-in-law about six months ago, asking for financial help. It seems that the son-in-law -notice I have not revealed any names here - has been unable to work as a result of a painful back injury. He is a bulldozer operator for a large construction company and is slowly recovering, but not yet to the degree where he can return to work.

The two of them came to Father Clayborne asking for guidance in the matter and, most of all, seeking any financial assistance that the parish might be able to supply. Father Clayborne gave them a cheque for five hundred dollars from his discretionary fund, and promised to do so for a six-month period until the husband should be back earning a wage.

Father Clayborne has made good on his promise to date, but the monies in his fund have been running low , so to make up the promised needed amount, he has been topping up the required amount with monies from his own savings account. He even brought in records of each cheque given to the needy family. That is the reason he has been requesting extra funds from the congregation each month. Of course, the Sallows have no idea that it is their own family members who are benefiting from Father Clayborne's noble pastoral solution to the temporary needs of a hurting family."

Bishop Strictman leaned back again in his chair and concluded, "This is the most encouraging story from one of my priests that I've heard in months. If only there were more like him!"

The three others sitting around the table were speechless. They had been totally unprepared for what Bishop Strictman had told them.

Finally, James Hunter, the more aggressive of the two Diocesan lawyers, broke the silence: "Bishop, we can't let the Sallows get away with this! They must be somehow made aware of the gravity of releasing their claim against Father Clayborne. Can you imagine how they may fare if they do go to the media, accuse Father Clayborne of misappropriation of funds, and the truth comes out in court that the monies were actually going to support their own family which they themselves have totally rejected?"

Bishop Strictman replied, "This is exactly why I have called you here today. We have to find a solution that doesn't totally humiliate the Sallows, and at the same time does not reveal how Father Clayborne used the discretionary funds. Remember, I gave him my word that outside of the four of us, everything he is doing is confidential."

"And," spoke up David McKnight, "somehow get the estranged parties back together as they should be in the first place. If the members of the parish were to learn the truth, why the Sallows could be completely ostracized in that closely knit parish!"

"Any suggestions?' asked Bishop Strictman.

The committee tossed around suggestions that might solve the dispute. Nothing seemed to surface that would ensure confidentiality of Father Joseph's dealings with the destitute young family and ending the Sallows' accusations of wrongdoing. To make the matter even more complex, there was the issue of the Sallows' rejection of the new son-in-law and their granddaughter. The matter must not, they all agreed, be allowed to continue to fester. And even more importantly, the Sallows must not under any circumstances publicly release their accusations against Father Clayborne.

Finally, it was James Hunter who offered his advice. "Bishop," he said, "I think that you ought to call Father Clayborne and instruct him to immediately contact the family, informing them that they must write a letter to the Sallows. In the letter they should ask the Sallows to join with them to meet their new granddaughter. Secondly, they need to inform the Sallows of their financial problems and how they would never have survived without Father Clayborne's financial assistance. How could the Sallows refuse such an invitation?"

"But what if the Sallows do refuse to meet with their family members?" inquired the Bishop. "Don't forget, I'm supposed to keep Father Clayborne's conversation with me confidential."

"Then Father Clayborne must first be instructed to meet with the Sallows, and then you Bishop, in your office, to bring to the surface what is behind the matter. Father Joseph will be exonerated, the Sallows will learn of the falsehood of their accusations, and then, indeed, their responsibility as parents to own their estranged son-in-law and granddaughter. This will save them from the disgrace of publically making false accusations and then the humiliation of trying to save face in the parish."

"How shall I hold off the Sallows from going to the public before Father Joseph and the young family write that letter and the Sallows receive it?" the Bishop asked. "They might be so ready to go public that the letter arrives too late?"

"Simple, Bishop," offered Hunter. "Call the Sallows and tell them you have received their letter and have a solution that will completely fix the matter, so to speak. They will be so pleased that you are on top of it, that they won't go public until they meet with you! Then the truth is out and they won't dare to follow up with their trumped up story. To stall for time, tell then that you can't meet with them for at least two weeks.

"Do you all agree?" grinned Bishop Strictman.

It was unanimous.

Mary Baldwin was instructed to mail minutes of the meeting to each of the three participants and to file a copy with the Bishop's personal records.

Harry's return trip in his new Audi was one of relief. There perhaps ought not to be a need for him to have to deal with the press over the Sallow's misinformed claims. Now to keep the Audi close to the posted speed limit.

Chapter Nine

THE three clergy next met for lunch at St. Bartholomew's with Canon Matthew providing the simple luncheon. The ladies' auxiliary group was kind enough to provide sandwiches and tomato and macaroni soup for the main meal, and vanilla ice cream for dessert. Tea, coffee, and orange juice were available as well. Canon Matthew, as the host, said grace before the meal began.

It was surprising how easily the three found common ground within their perspective Christian denominations. Canon Matthew agreed to act as the scribe, jotting down on a flip chart with coloured markers their brainstorming proposals. No order of commentary was ranked in the process. They agreed that sorting through the growing list would take place later on. The list grew fast and enthusiastically:

"All Christians, no matter their denomination, believe in God, in Jesus Christ as God's only son, the Virgin Mary, the Holy Scriptures as the revealed word of God, original sin, the power of prayer, the need of organized worship, salvation, heaven and hell, Baptism and Holy Communion."

There was no dispute what-so-ever between any of the three clergy-men. This list was so obvious that Father Leo commented, "Doesn't every lay person out there know these facts?"

"No, they don't," offered Angus. "They only focus on how we differ, not on what we universally hold in common. That's why it is so neces-sary for the Church to articulate our denominational similarities. In the modern age, vast numbers of men and women, totally unfamiliar with orthodox belief act as their own theologians."

"But don't they know the creeds? It's all there, summarized centu-ries ago!" interjected Father Leo.

"The vast majority of modern Christian denominations never say the creed during public worship," replied Canon Matthew. "Outside Roman Catholicism, the Orthodox Churches, the Anglicans and the Lutherans, creeds are seldom, if ever, recited."

"Why not?" asked Father Leo.

"Because the creeds include four words that the vast majority of Christians refuse to say: the words 'the Holy Catholic Church.'"

"Don't they know the meaning of the word 'catholic'? All it means is the 'universal,' the church from the beginning, the church embrac-ing the whole body of Christians, theological fundamentals agreed upon by the early church fathers and the great councils of the past," responded Father Leo.

"Of course that's what the word means," agreed Canon Matthew. "But since the time of the Protestant Reformation, somehow many of the reformers rejected the word 'catholic' because it was, in their minds, associated with Roman Catholicism. So to distance them-selves, they dropped the perfectly good and useful term. To all of Christendom's detriment, I might add!"

"You see gentlemen," smiled Doctor Angus, "that is entirely the point I've been trying to make to Harry Sting on his show. Christians divided among themselves, straining at a gnat while swallowing a camel! Fighting, while the secular world points their fingers at us and asks, if they are so divided, why would anyone be interested in choosing to follow their teachings? Get your own house in order before you come preaching to us!"

"Do you, Angus, use the creed in your services?" asked Father Leo.

"Not as often as we should, Leo. I'm afraid we Presbyterians have some work to do in our churches. But that is going to change at St. Andrew's, I can tell you that."

"So what are we going to do about Harry Sting's invitation to be guests on an upcoming show?" a frustrated Father Leo inquired.

"I think it is simply a matter of appearing together on Sting's show, getting him to ask what all Christians agree on when it comes to standard Christian doctrine, and one-by-one, we each take turns reading the Nicene Creed one line at a time. Then wait for the fun to begin in the second portion, the call-in," grinned Canon Matthew.

"Brilliant," agreed Father Leo.

"Let's do it!" agreed Doctor Angus. "It seems that our work has been done for us way back at the time of the Council of Nicaea in the year 325 AD. How in the world could any Christian today dispute their deliberations? Besides, it will give us a great opportunity to teach a little church history to those listeners who may not know about that Council."

"Will you set it up for us with Harry then?"

"Sure will, Leo. What a productive meeting this first one has been for us. Say the benediction Father, and we'll call it a day."

Now to bring Harry Sting up to date, thought Angus as he drove back to his office.

Chapter Ten

THE three clerics arrived early for the Monday AM KNOW Harry Sting Show. Harry welcomed them warmly and offered them coffee as they were ushered to his office. He was demonstrably excited.

"Let's quickly run through our approach, shall we gentlemen?" Harry suggested. "How do you want me to broach the theme of our show this morning?"

Doctor Angus spoke up for the other two who had agreed that he would be the lead-in for the show. They had agreed that they would take turns, when the opportunity was sensed, to read the words of the Nicene Creed and convey their intentions to Harry.

Harry was already formulating in his mind the approach he would take to lead the three into their pre-arranged plan. They explained to Harry that some versions of the Nicene Creed began with the word 'I.' Because the three were making a united claim, they would use the version of the creed that begins with the collective word 'we'. "We believe". "Sounds great, friends. Remember that the show is only half an hour long with a couple of commercial breaks. Time passes so quickly that we'll be finished before you know it. How do you want to be introduced at the beginning?"

"Use our proper titles, naming our individual churches, along with our denominational affiliations," answered Father Leo. "Right from the beginning we want to convey to your audience that we are together on the show, united in what we will say, Christians first and foremost even though our worship styles may differ."

"Got it!" replied Harry. "Let's go over to the control room and get ready. I've instructed our crew to make sure that there are enough chairs in there to accommodate all of you as guests. Bring your coffee with you."

"Oh, and Harry," interjected Angus, "when the time seems right to you, ask us about the phrase 'the Holy Catholic Church.' We are ready to answer what it means. But be prepared to field questions in your second half of the show from those who will certainly object to its use."

Harry grinned. "Love it! Can't wait for the fireworks!" A little of the old Harry Sting was clearly still there, just below the surface.

The technician in the control room was holding up his hand: five fingers, then four, then three, two, one.

"Good morning, thinking people of Tangleville, and a warm welcome to you, the listening audience. Have I got a show lined up for you to-day! My guests are here because of a statement made by the Reverend Canon Doctor Barclay Steadmore a few weeks ago. You will remember him: he was the former rector of St. Bartholomew's Anglican parish here in Tangleville. And do you remember what it was that he said on the show that day? He said, and I'm going to paraphrase his words: 'The greatest scandal in the world is the scandal, the divide, that separates Christians. Christians fight amongst themselves, he said. Christians can't even get along with one another. It's a disgrace, he told us.

Well that statement stirred up our town! It has ignited three of the most prominent clergy of our community who are here this morning to support Doctor Steadmore's claims.

Welcome to Doctor Angus McLaughlin, minister at St. Andrew's Presbyterian Church, Father Leo Mahoney, rector of St. Anne's Roman Catholic Parish, and Canon Matthew Hudson, the successor of Canon Doctor Steadmore over at St. Bart's Anglican Church. I'm assuming that you are here to agree with Steadmore's accusations? Am I right?"

Angus - the appointed point-man for the three - replied, "We most certainly are Mr. Sting. In fact, we were so concerned about Doctor Steadmore's accusations, that we've met over lunch and are committed to working together, all three denominations, to prove to Christians in Tangleville that our three denominations have far more in common than that which separates us. And I suspect that there will be many of your listeners who will agree with us, but have never in the past felt it necessary to say it publicly or to demonstrate that Christianity is worried about how secular society views us."

"So gentlemen of the cloth," Harry said, "convince me and my audience that your three denominations share orthodox Christian beliefs - traditional, standard theological teachings from the beginning of Christian doctrine - and are not rivals of one another. This I've got to hear!"

Harry was leaning past his microphone, grinning widely as he waited for the three to respond to his invitation for them to rehearse their response to this expected question.

The three were waiting and ready for this exact moment. It was previously agreed as to the order in which they would answer: first Angus, then Matthew, and thirdly Leo. Harry was not to interrupt their shared response.

Angus began, emphasizing the word 'We".

"*We* believe in one God,

The Father, the Almighty,

maker of heaven and earth,

of all that is, seen and unseen."

Not giving Harry time to inject a single word, Matthew continued clearly articulating the word 'We'.,

"*We* believe in one Lord, Jesus Christ,

the only Son of God,

eternally begotten of the Father,

God from God, Light from Light,

true God from true God,

begotten not made,

of one being with the Father.

Through him all things were made.

For us and for our salvation he came down from heaven:

by the power of the Holy Spirit

he became incarnate from the Virgin Mary,

and was made man.

For our sake he was crucified

under Pontius Pilate;

he suffered death and was buried.

On the third day he rose again

in accordance with the scriptures;

he ascended into heaven

and is seated at the right hand of the Father.

He will come again in glory

to judge the living and the dead,

and his kingdom will have no end."

Then it was Leo's turn.

"*We* believe in the Holy Spirit,

the Lord, the giver of life,

who proceeds from the Father.

With the Father and the Son

he is worshipped and glorified.

He has spoken through the prophets.

We believe in one holy catholic

and apostolic Church.

We acknowledge one baptism

for the forgiveness of sins.

We look for the resurrection of the dead,

and the life of the world to come. Amen."

The three then sat in silence, a rather lengthy period of dead air time.

Finally, Harry spoke: "Why, you have just read out the words of the Nicene Creed. Why in the world did you do that?"

"Because, Mr. Sting," replied Father Leo, "back at the Council of Nicaea in A.D. 325, the Church leaders, relatively undivided at the time, agreed on the fundamentals of Christianity. For many Christians today, those fundamentals have not changed. Not one iota.

The creed covers the major themes of Christianity. God the Father, creator of the universe, Jesus, God's Son, born of a virgin, His crucifixion and His resurrection, the promise of His second coming, the continuing presence of the Holy Spirit to be with the church and individual believers.

Of course, we Christians believe in the Bible, and tradition, sin, salvation, forgiveness, the sacraments, the necessity of organized worship, heaven and hell. Of course, we Christians may differ in how these fundamentals may be addressed, their design and use of liturgy, music and discipleship. But no one, no member of Christianity would dispute the statement that Jesus Christ is the path to truth, for He said in St. John, Chapter 14:6, 'I am the way, the truth and the life. No one comes to the Father except through me.'"

"But Father," said Harry, "the creed makes the statement that seems to divide Christians, the words, 'one holy, catholic, and apostolic Church.' Surely you must agree that all Christians can't say those words, can you?"

"Of course they can Mr. Sting. All the word 'catholic' means is that conveyed by the modern word 'universal,' meaning what was held in common everywhere in AD 325, that which was agreed upon by the Church Fathers. The term 'catholic' at the time simply meant 'universal' acceptance.

"So you're saying the holy catholic church statement does not only apply to the Roman Catholic, Anglican, or Orthodox Churches?

"Right on, Mr. Sting," responded Father Leo. "All Christians are part of the Holy Catholic Church and ought to proclaim it universally."

"Well Doctor McLaughlin, as a Presbyterian, can you claim to be part of one holy catholic church?"

"Absolutely," replied Angus. "And proudly so!"

"So why then don't all the Christian denominations use the same liturgy in worship?" inquired Harry.

"We come from different cultures, different languages and customs, vastly different ways to relate to the Divine," replied Canon Hudson. "Some people worship primarily through the use of their senses: let me call it heart-felt experiential, emotional worship. Others are 'head' people, rational, the mind over emotion to encounter God. We are all different, but at the same time, all share the common need to bow before the Almighty in worship. We pay our spiritual taxes, so to speak, in different ways."

The On Air portion of the show was interrupted by two commercials. During the break, the four quickly assessed how they were coming across to the listening audience. Harry was obviously pleased and, just before the On Air sign was about to light, said, "Keep it up fellows. The call-in section is going to be a sideshow!"

The final few minutes of the show was a time for all four to continue to discuss what the three clerics called the incidentals of Christianity: the types of prayers used during the liturgy: formal versus spontaneous, chants, hand clapping during hymns, modern versus traditional, organ music versus guitars and drums.

Canon Matthew and Father Leo were in agreement that in the presence of a Holy God, both their denominations felt obligated to employ eloquent and grammatically correct, dignified language during the liturgy. After all, the people were gathered before God Almighty.

"If one," they argued, "would expect such protocol before dignitaries and royalty, surely one would do so before the King of Kings!"

"Others may disagree," they continued, "and feel that it is perfectly acceptable to express their emotions and joyful admiration for God in less formal ways."

"Incidentals," Doctor Angus reminded them. "Incidentals! But we do not, as Christians, disagree on the fundamentals of Christian doctrine. There is no scandal there!"

Harry closed the show by thanking all three of his guests, naming them in turn and again identifying their denominations and parish names.

The three clergy embraced and, after thanking Harry, decided to meet for coffee at the local coffee shop to debrief following the show. It would be good for people to see the three socializing in public.

CHAPTER ELEVEN

OVER coffee at The Bean Grinder the three clerics were busy planning their next move. They agreed that it would be prudent to wait for Harry Sting to give them a brief summary of how things transpired during the second portion of the show, the call-in opportunity for his listeners to comment on what was discussed during the previous thirty minute group presentation. The three were clearly elated over their joint claim of unity when it came to the fundamentals of Christianity.

"Why don't we use the opportunity to further push our claims in print?" asked Angus. "Don't forget that I write a regular Monday column in The Mirror. What would you say if I focus on the topic of Christian disunity and division in my next article?"

Father Leo was all for it. "Before you send it to the press, email your article to Matthew and myself so that if anyone asks if we were in agreement, we can truthfully say we are," he suggested.

"Would it be beneficial if we all had our names included in this article so that the readers will then know that your submission is group sanctioned?" inquired Matthew.

It was unanimous: Angus would return to his office and put ink to paper. He could hardly wait to let his enthusiasm be expressed in print. It would be a more potent submission than usual because of the inclusion of the names of the other two clerics. Hard copy trumps the spoken word every time!

On returning to his office at St. Andrews, Angus settled behind his desk before his computer with a fresh cup of coffee. He had instructed Heather to give him a two-hour interval for writing uninterrupted, if possible. She could handle all non-urgent situations and take notes for him to follow up later in the day.

For an academic, writing is one of life's greatest joys. Angus began to formulate his thoughts to challenge his readership in the next edition of The Mirror. It would not be aimed at his usual readership, rather it would be directed to Christian brothers and sisters in Christ. He knew that his article would have to be upfront so that non-Christians would not take offense to this week's column.

THE CLERIC SPEAKS
by The Rev. Dr. Angus McLaughlin

Dear people of Tangleville: This week's column is intended for a limited audience: all folks who call themselves Christian. I do not want in any way to upset my non-Christian readers; this is certainly not my intention.

But we Christians have a problem that needs to be addressed in this new decade of the 21st Century: the scandal of division that separates us from one another.

Consider the following passage from the Gospel of John. Jesus is praying for His disciples and the church. He is worried about divisions that may slip into their ministry following His resurrection. He says to His Father:

"*I ask not only on behalf of these, but also on behalf of those who will believe in me through their word, that they may all be one.*" (John 17:20)

"*The glory that you have given me I have given them so that they may be* one, *I in them and you in me, that they may become completely one …*" (John 17:22)

St. Paul picks up the very same concern when he writes to Timothy, his faithful contemporary fellow missionary. He says:

"*I urge you, as I did when I was on my way to Macedonia, to remain in Ephesus so that you may instruct certain people not to teach any different doctrine.* " (I Timothy 1:3)

In St. Paul's letter, it is obvious that our Lord's concern for unity in the church was already being challenged. The point St. Paul is trying to make to Timothy is that disunity in doctrine destroys the Church's witness to the world!

Fast forward to today! Are you aware of how fractured the Christian Church is in our modern world? The World Christian Encyclopaedia in 2001 counted 33,830 divided versions of the Christian Church around the world, each claiming to be the true, authentic bearers of our Lord's message, the Good News of the Gospel. And to further give reason for concern, the article estimates that by the year 2025, there will be 55,000 separate bodies

each giving their interpretations of Christ's teachings.

I ask, was our Lord's message of the Good News of the Gospel that obscure, that complex, that nebulous, that His followers cannot fathom what He meant and taught during His three years of ministry? Surely not!

Yet, we continue to argue and disagree while called to be His witnesses, and then split off to go our separate ways, each claiming to possess the 'truth' of the Good News! No wonder the non-Christian world points its fingers and scoffs: "How do they expect us to take them seriously when they can't even agree amongst themselves as to what their founder taught?"

Well friends, they have a point, and we Christians have a problem. Let me put it even more bluntly: we are the heirs of the greatest scandal the world has ever witnessed!

Canon Matthew Hudson at St. Bartholomew's Anglican Parish, and Father Leo Mahoney at St. Anne's Roman Catholic Church are so concerned that we three have been meeting on a weekly basis to discuss means to diminish this perception of disunity within the Tangleville community. Both clerics have read this article before you and firmly give their consent to its content and pledge to work as a team to begin to present a common Christian witness in Tangleville.

Clergy and pastors of Tangleville, if you are concerned over the fracture of the contemporary Christian Church, we invite you to join the three of us as we work together to initiate a more unified voice in our community. We want to accentuate and affirm what we hold in common, the fundamentals of the faith, and minimize the incidentals that separate us.

Laity, pray for the church and encourage your clergy to become part of the team that in some small way, may eradicate the scandal which separates us as Christ's own. After all, Christ and St. Paul in Holy Scriptures have instructed us to do so!

All responses to this article can reach me by email to:

drangus@fastmail.com.

CHAPTER TWELVE

FATHER Clayborne knew that it would not be an easy meeting. He had been instructed by Bishop Strictman to set up an interview with the Sallows to try and bring the entire inflammatory conflict to a possible end. He was aware that the Sallows had it in for him as their parish priest. It was not the first time. They had been successful in causing two former priests to resign because the Sallows disagreed with their style of leadership. The congregation, reluctant to disagree with the Sallows, up to now, had never opposed their bullying tactics. But this time the Sallows had met their match. Father Clayborne had the backing of the Bishop, and he knew it!

The two parties agreed to meet in Father Clayborne's office. The time was set for seven o'clock on a Tuesday evening. Father Clayborne had the coffee pot on and a tray filled with muffins which his spouse Angela had prepared for the occasion.

The Sallows arrived twelve minutes late for the appointment, which Father Clayborne suspected was just another attempt to control the situation. To keep him waiting was a clear indication that they were not to be manipulated.

It was an uneasy first fifteen minutes. Coffee and muffins were shared around the large table in Clayborne's office, the very table that was used monthly for parish council meetings. Father Clayborne began the business part of the gathering by asking the Sallows to pause for a brief prayer in which he asked God's blessing upon the parish, the community and the meeting itself. The Sallows concluded the prayers with rather reluctant "amens."

Father Clayborne, always a man in charge, notified the Sallows that he was aware of the two letters which they had sent to Bishop Strictman. He immediately asked them for the *real* reason for sending such letters to the bishop.

Judy Sallow was the first to speak: "Because, Rev. Clayborne, we believe that you are misappropriating funds from your discretionary fund. No priest before you has ever requested such a large amount. Five hundred dollars a month is simply too much for our little parish to afford!"

"Is that it?" probed Father Clayborne. "Is it strictly a matter of money? Or is it that you don't trust how I spend that money?"

"Well," continued Judy, her voice getting shriller, "Jim and I can't help but notice that you are driving a new Subaru. We suspect that some of the parish money is being used for vehicle payments. Now we want to know if this is true." Judy sat back in her chair, arms crossed in a defiant manner, confident that she had cornered Father Clayborne.

"No, it's not true," he replied calmly. "Are you sure that that is your real beef with me? Is it simply a matter of money that has motivated your letters to Bishop Strictman?"

Judy and Jim were silent. Father Clayborne waited for their response. It seemed to take a full three-minute pause for Judy to compose herself. As usual, Jim was prepared for her to do all the talking.

Father Clayborne broke the silence: "There is something else, isn't there?" You don't approve of my worship style, do you? You think that I'm 'high church.' Why don't you come out and admit it?"

"Well, you are, and Jim and I don't like that! So what are you going to do about it? Our two former rectors wouldn't listen to us and they both resigned. We think that you should too!"

Father Joseph didn't answer their accusations. He leaned back in his chair and calmly began his response. "What I'm going to say to you this evening may be very difficult for you to hear. But as your priest, and with the full approval of Bishop Strictman, I must do so."

Judy's eyes were blazing and her lips were firmly compressed. Jim appeared agitated, but it was becoming clear that he was merely a puppet in his wife's presence. He looked extremely uncomfortable as he waited for Father Joseph to continue.

"Before your arrival this evening, Jim and Judy, I want you to know that I was given permission to reveal facts that may cause you great concern - even sorrow. Information, may I add, that will hurt you deeply. This permission to do so has been granted by your daughter and your son-in-law to whom, I've learned, you have refused to speak to for over a two-year period. They both know that I am meeting with you tonight, and have asked that I break some news to you as gently as I can possibly do so."

Joseph waited with a lengthy pause, giving the Sallows an opportunity to respond. Neither of them uttered a word.

"Your daughter, and her husband whom you have never met since their marriage, nor accepted as part of your family, and your grand-daughter Grace, now well over a year old, are in deep financial trouble. Art, Joy's husband, is on a disability pension following a severe accident at work and benefits are about to end. Well over six months ago, they approached me asking if there was any way I might give them some financial assistance. They were far behind in credit card payments, even lacking in such bare necessities as grocery money. Fortunately, I have access to funds which I was able to dip into: the rector's discretionary fund. I've been supplying them with eight hundred dollars a month since their first visit to my office."

Father Joseph paused deliberately, waiting to see how the Sallows would respond to the revelation.

Jim took out a rather well-used handkerchief and wiped tears streaming down his cheeks. Father Clayborne, without uttering a word, pushed a box of Kleenex toward the extremely troubled man. Jim pulled out a handful of tissues, stood up and walked to the far corner of the office, finally sitting down in a chair which he moved to face the office wall, his back to Judy and the rector. Judy refused to utter a single word.

Father Clayborne, facing Judy, asked, "Do you need me to give you more information? Now have you begun to understand why I have been asking the parish for an increase in discretionary funds?"

Judy still did not utter a sole word in response to the rector's questions.

Father Joseph felt he needed to continue:

"As for the purchase of my new Subaru, you might be interested in knowing that a distant relative of mine, a single aunt living in

California, died and left me a very large inheritance. I've invested the major portion of that money, but splurged on the SUV. And that is how I've been able to make up the extra three hundred dollars to top up St. Hilda's-in-the-Fields' monthly donation to my discretionary fund. I've just taken a little from my inheritance to supplement your family's needs to make it eight hundred a month."

"Joy defied my wishes to marry Art," was all Judy was willing to reply.

Jim jumped to his feet and returned to stand by his chair, beside Judy.

"Judy, for heaven's sake, it's time to let it go! I've heard enough, and I can't stand it any longer! I'm going over to our family's home tonight, and I'm taking my cheque book. You can come with me or you can stay at home. It's time to live up to our proclaimed Christian values and responsibilities. Are you coming or not?"

Father Clayborne wisely knew that it was time for him to spend private confidential time with Judy.

"Jim," he said, "please step out of my office into the waiting room for a few minutes. I need to talk with Judy one-on-one. You can watch us through that window."

Jim, box in hand, took another handful of tissues and moved next door to sit on a large leather chair directly facing the window dividing the two rooms.

Finally, Judy let down her hardened facade and blurted out: "I've never really loved Joy like Jim does. She was conceived three months before we were married, and I wanted to get an abortion before our big wedding day. Jim wouldn't hear of it. To this day I've regretted her birth!"

Judy confessed her resentment towards Jim and Joy's intrusion in her life, and that she had lost control when she couldn't talk her daughter out of marrying Art. Joy went against her mother's wishes and married the man she loved, and for many years, Judy had let these disappointments eat away at her. To make matters even more uncomfortable, Jim had been pressing her to submit and make amends with Joy and her husband. Now he was going to do so, with or without her.

Finally, when Joseph thought it was time to sum it up, he said, "Judy, you've got a husband you ought to be proud of, and let me tell you a wonderful daughter and son-in-law and granddaughter who are just waiting - praying in fact - to be accepted. This is the parable of the Prodigal Son in reverse."

Grinning, he leaned forward and continued, "I'll bet my new SUV that they will welcome you with open arms, just as the father in the parable welcomed home his wayward repentant son. Go with Jim and bury your hostility, and your pride, and throw your arms around your God-given family members!"

Judy, at last, let down her guard and the tears began to flow.

"Jim!" the rector called. "Come back in here and bring that box of Kleenex!"

Judy threw her arms around Jim and sobbed, "I'm going with you, we're going tonight. Are you sure that you have your cheque book on you?"

Jim, in typical fashion, agreed with his spouse even though he knew that it was through his own doing that the ice was broken.

Father Clayborne held Jim's and Judy's hands and prayed a blessing upon the upcoming family meeting. This was a prayer that Father Joseph was certain would be answered.

Judy and Jim, arm-in-arm, walked to their expensive Dodge Ram 4 x 4 pick-up out in the parish parking lot. Jim was a half-step ahead of Judy.

Isn't it interesting, Father Joseph thought to himself. Judy never even mentioned her 'high church' disapproval of liturgy in her time of confession with me. I guess it really wasn't the root of the problem with the former two rectors, or himself, after all, he mused. One has to probe beneath the surface to discover the real causes of irritation submerged by time itself.

CHAPTER THIRTEEN

THE three downtown clergy had agreed that they would meet over lunch every second Wednesday in order to devise a plan to unite Tangleville Christian clerics so that as many denominations as possible may be encouraged to work together to provide a more integrated voice in the community.

Following their joint presentation on the Harry Sting Show and after talking with Harry about his assessment of the call-in section, the three were most encouraged over how the majority of listeners applauded their plea for a common Christian voice in their town. They had invited Harry to the luncheon to strategize and to work with them in formulating their next steps.

The meeting was hosted by Father Leo at St. Anne's, with the parish providing a light lunch for the occasion. They were surprised and somewhat unprepared when three other prominent clergy also showed up for the meeting: Major John Huff from the downtown Salvation Army Citadel, the Reverend Charles MacCormick from the First Baptist Church, and Father Ivan Fedosov, Rector of St. Nicholas' Russian Orthodox Parish, the parish where Annie Sting regularly worshipped. Annie, it seemed, had told Father Ivan about the meeting at St. Anne's and strongly encouraged him to attend. He had not heard the presentation of the three on the Sting Show, but had read with interest Doctor Angus' article in the Tangleville Mirror.

Harry, of course, knew Father Ivan because of Annie's membership at St. Nicholas' and introduced the gathered clergy to one another. The only problem for Father Leo was whether or not he had enough soup and dessert to go around. There was, but not quite sufficient for second helpings!

They all agreed that they had better be more prepared for a future meeting. Father Leo had blessed the meal before they ate, and joked that if Christ had been there He would have done what He had done with the loaves and fishes at the time of the feeding of the five thousand. Reverend MacCormick chimed in and suggested that there may be indeed such a time in Tangleville to accommodate a gathering of that many modern Christians if their joint plans for unity were to become a reality.

Harry made a presentation summarizing what he concluded was the overall response the listening audience had made during the call in section of the show following Angus, Leo, and Matthew's presentation. Surprisingly, he reported, the vast majority were in complete agreement with the words of the Nicene Creed which the three had read in its entirety. Many had said that they had heard of the creed, but did not recite it in public worship and wondered why it was not used in their denominations. A very few belligerent callers were in total disagreement with the plea for a common Christian voice in the community. "We don't want any religion of any kind shoved down our throats," one caller said. "Leave us alone! When people unite, they become intrusive! Keep those Christians at odds with one another and let them fight amongst themselves!"

Harry finished his summary of the call-in section with a direct quotation from one of his female listeners: "It's time the clergy of Tangleville mobilized their congregations to work together and to present a unified Christian voice in our community. I say, lets 'step out' together and strive as St. Paul instructed the church to do in First Thessalonians, Chapter Five, verse 13: to 'be at peace amongst yourselves.'"

"Well if we ever needed a slogan, that woman gave us one," responded Major Huff. "'Stepping Out' is a loaded phrase."

The seven gathered men nodded to each other in agreement.

"That's it! replied Angus. "What say we adopt it as our mantra for future combined activities?"

"Do you think that the two words 'stepping out' could be somehow integrated into a crest, or let's say a pin on lapel button to be worn by our people - one that uses Christian symbols, but not depicting a specific Christian denomination?" asked Father Leo.

"Why don't you agree to let me inform my readers in my next article in the Tangleville Voice that we have come up with a logo for Christian cooperation and invite my readers to submit a design for such a catch phrase? There are some pretty talented people out there!"

"Let's go for it," responded Matthew.

There was total agreement around the table. Harry and the six clerics agreed to meet again in two weeks at the Salvation Army Citadel downtown. Major Huff promised that there would be plenty of soup available to satisfy their appetites. "After all," he joked, "we hold soup kitchen luncheons on every Wednesday noon hour."

In the meantime, the clerics were charged to return to their parishes and begin to set up information sharing with their laity and to brainstorm how 'stepping out' would be implicated in a unified and spirit fueled positive fashion in their town. At the next meeting, their suggestions would be shared and evaluated.

"Harry, say hello to Annie for me", requested Father Ivan. "She is one special lady."

"Don't I know it, Father," grinned Harry. "She has to be to have agreed to marry me! And by the way, I'll put a notice over the air on my show that our next meeting will be at the Salvation Army Citadel, and that all Christian clergy in the town are invited to attend. Can you handle that Major?"

"The Salvation Army has never been known to turn anyone away!" quipped Major Huff. "We can handle it!"

Chapter Fourteen

ANGUS spent the next morning working on his upcoming Friday publication in the Tangleville Mirror. It took him three hours to write and to proof read the article, which needed to be submitted the Wednesday before the Friday publication.

THE CLERIC SPEAKS

By The Rev. Dr. Angus McLaughlin

You need to know that something of importance is brewing in Tangleville, something that will have pronounced consequences for our community! As I informed you in a previous article, Christian clergy in our town are determined to give our Christian community a common, unified presence and voice in our secular town. Along with myself, Father Leo Mahoney of St. Anne's Roman Catholic Parish and Canon Matthew Hudson over at St. Bartholomew's Anglican Parish, we have been gathering to devise strategy to bring our now divided Christian communities into an organized presence to better share the Good News of the Gospel.

The aim is to celebrate what we share in common, but leaving individual denominations to adhere to their own particular forms of church liturgies during times of worship. The fact is that we share more in common than that which divides and separates us. It has been far too long that we have been judged to be at odds with each other. This is simply not the fact when we closely examine our fundamental beliefs and mandates for mission.

Now, three more prominent Tangleville clergy have joined our ranks: Major John Huff of the Salvation Army Citadel, The Reverend Charles MacCormick of downtown First Baptist Church, and Father Ivan Fedosov, rector of St. Nicholas' Russian Orthodox Parish. We met last Wednesday during the noon hour and almost ran out of food for the luncheon meeting. One can only conclude that we are a hungry group … not only for nourishment for the body, but also for spiritual growth and mission.

We now introduce something that you have a need to hear and a need to respond … the new slogan unanimously agreed upon by the growing clergy co-operative: Stepping Out.

In the coming days, Tangleville parishes and the community at large are going to hear about this challenge over and over again: Stepping Out.

What does 'stepping out' mean? Clearly that expression will be our evolving challenge in future days as Christians discover opportunities to do so. This is precisely where we need the readers of this article to respond. You are invited to submit suggestions where and when Christians may come together and demonstrate unity to proclaim the message of Christ to our community. The aim is not to be aggressive or threatening to secular society. The aim is not to be in anyone's face, so to speak. But rather, to witness to the love of Christ to those who do not know of His message. This is not a plan for all Christian denominations to eventually become one in liturgical worship nor theological doctrinal positions. It is, however, as some have put it, unity in diversity. We believe that each denomination and each individual Christian possesses unique God-given gifts, which when shared together, can be far more effective in ministry than when divided denominations attempt to do so in isolation.

I put it to you: How do you envision our Churches working together, proclaiming the Good News to Tangleville? You are invited to suggest projects, undertakings, ventures, businesses, even joint public gatherings, perhaps during such high feast days as Palm Sunday and Easter, to share in common. Add to this list and email me with your creative ideas. I will pass them on to the other members of the committee.

And Tangleville Christian clergy, there is an open invitation to you to come to a meeting scheduled for the Wednesday after next, to be hosted by Major Huff at the downtown Salvation Army Citadel. Remember, Jesus recruited twelve disciples. Our number is now at seven!

All responses to this article can reach me by email at:

drangus@fastmail.com.

With his article completed, he was free to make his hospital rounds downtown. Doing so on a regular basis is one of the most important roles of a clergyperson's ministry. To visit the bedside of the sick, sometimes the dying, is a sacred privilege. When people are ill, it's a time of complete honesty with clergy, time when one's faith in God is discovered to be more important than anything else in life. Doctor Angus knew that he could never predict how long such visits may take him when he did his hospital chaplaincy visits. Today would prove to be no exception to the rule!

CHAPTER FIFTEEN

MAJOR Huff was looking forward to hosting the Wednesday meeting at the downtown Citadel. The menu for the day for the regular one hundred or so drop-ins of Tangleville was vegetable and rice or mushroom soup, ham or tuna sandwiches, dessert, tea, coffee and orange juice.

He was always appreciative of the fifteen volunteers who gathered every noon to prepare the meal and do the clean-up following the event. The day would be an important one, as Harry Sting and the six downtown clerics were coming for their noon hour meeting. They would be sharing the same menu as the daily drop-in folks who met at the Citadel. Major Huff had forewarned his chef that he really didn't know how many other clergy, not yet members of the growing consortium, might show up. The chef put the Major at ease. He could handle it, he assured the officer.

Harry Sting and Fr. Leo were the first to arrive. As they waited for Canon Matthew, Dr. Angus, Rev. Charles and Father Ivan, Major Huff offered them tea or coffee, as they engaged in conversation, each giving a brief rundown of their perspective thoughts during the past two weeks. It was evident that Harry and Father Leo were becoming close friends.

All six were preparing to be seated when one of Major Huff's staff ushered in three more individuals, obviously clergy of Tangleville: one wearing a sharp business suit with a well-coordinated tie; one wearing a clerical collar; the third immaculately dressed in a grey ladies jacket and skirt.

Major Huff made introductions all around as he was well aware of the identity of the arrivals. He had previously met each of them as their congregations were regular donors to the financial needs of the Citadel. There was the Reverend Mary Jones of the downtown Pentecostal Assemblies; Pastor Richard Head of Tangleville's huge Community Church on the outskirts of the town, a non-denominational evangelical congregation with a ten-acre parking lot needed for their growing membership; and the Reverend Dieter Muller, rector of St. Peter's Lutheran Church in the center of Tangleville.

Remaining standing, the nine clerics and Harry gathered around a large dining room table. Major Huff said a short blessing for the meal, and the volunteers were waiting to serve their guests as each lined up cafeteria style to receive their lunch. It was a far cry from the service one might receive in one of Tangleville's posh downtown restaurants.

Major Huff reminded his guests that the menu for the day was similar to meals served daily at the Citadel. He shocked some of his guests when he told them that the noon-hour meal was likely to be the only one that many of the drop-ins would receive for the day. Major Huff couldn't admit it aloud, but he had an ulterior motive in mind: to plant seeds in the minds of the Stepping Out organizers to help keep his food bank shelves well stocked.

Dr. Angus chaired the meeting following the plain, but adequate luncheon. He began by inviting each of the nine clerics to give a brief summary of their ministries, and to include the reasons why they were motivated to possibly enlist in their town's fast growing movement for a common Christian voice. He was particularly interested in learning whether or not each clergy's laity were behind their leaders joining such a diverse alliance.

This exercise took approximately twenty-five minutes to complete. What surprised most of the gathered clergy was that it was actually the laity in their respective denominations who had encouraged their clergy to get involved. Many had read Dr. Angus' article in the Tangleville Mirror and quite a few had listened in to the Harry Sting Show, stating that they were moved to overcome their denominational differences to speak out as a unified voice in their town.

Many of the laity had suggested ideas for co-operation in such an undertaking with one person suggesting the clerics entitle the movement The Tangleville Christian Coalition.

Dr. Angus acted as the scribe, and using a flip chart jotted down each of the diverse suggestions which the clergy and their laity wanted to be included in a future communique. In no particular order, the ideas came fast and furious:

- The theme of Christian love
- Respect for the Sabbath
- Joint parades down the streets of Tangleville
- Interdenominational sports events
- The formation of a multi-denominational help line
- A giant Easter egg hunt
- The sharing of parish announcements between denominations
- The formation of an interdenominational band to play at church functions

— No duplication of services such as food banks, clothing depots, etc. Each denomination should support whichever parish was already doing exceptional work in such areas

— Sharing prayer lists for the sick, the needy, and the afflicted

— Co-operation, not competition, wherever possible

The list continued to grow, and it became obvious to the clerics around the lunch table that the laity in the various congregations were well past isolationism and willing and eager to work together in their town. The question arose: Are we as Christian leaders willing to do likewise? Can we put our denominational differences aside and, for the sake of the Gospel, work together in a new twenty-first century non-partisan fashion?

"If we are going to be stepping out together to become the Tangleville Christian Coalition then we don't have any choice, do we?" Reverend Mary Jones volunteered. "I'm all for it!"

Ever the articulate one, the word craftsman of the group, Dr. Angus, suggested that each of the clergy return to their parish office, and in the next couple of days submit to him by email what each felt must go into a joint statement mandate, maybe even calling it a manifesto, a summary of clear statements for publication to Tangleville.

Major Huff gave the final blessing and the nine clerics dispersed from the meeting. There had certainly been enough food to go around for the luncheon meeting, and more than enough provisions for future plans of the highly motivated church leaders.

On their way to the parking lot, Canon Matthew and Father Leo walked side by side.

"Canon," Father Leo said, "did you ever expect to see the day when all those different denominational churches would agree to work together for the good of the Kingdom?"

"No, Father," grinned Canon Matthew. "Maybe the Psalmist's words in Psalm 118: 'This is the Lord's doing, it is marvellous in our eyes. This is the day that the Lord has made; let us rejoice and be glad in it' are finally being taken seriously!"

"Bless you Father" replied Father Leo. "We can't hold back the will of God."

Chapter Sixteen

OVER the next three days, Dr. Angus received twenty-one emails from the clerics who'd attended the luncheon at the downtown Salvation Army Citadel. Some were brief in nature, recorded in point form, while others were lengthy, written in almost a scholarly fashion. Each suggested ideas possibly to be included in their joint release to the Christian Churches and the townsfolk of Tangleville.

Dr. Angus was now faced with the consequential task of sorting through the submissions in order to compose a statement that could be signed by each of the participating clergy - no small undertaking - keeping in mind that liturgical and theological denominational differences needed to be respected.

His thoughts could not help but be drawn back to one of the most influential manifestos of the twentieth century: the words of The Reverend Doctor Martin Luther King, when he said,

"I have a dream that one day this nation will rise up and live out the true meaning of its creed: we hold these truths to be self-evident, that all men are created equal.

I have a dream that one day on the red hills of Georgia the sons of former slaves and the sons of former slave owners will be able to sit down together at the table of brotherhood."

Why not adopt Doctor King's words to fit the modern day situation in Tangleville? he reasoned. King's words were about to change those troubled times - to rewrite the future! Surely Doctor King would not object, McLaughlin thought, to being plagiarized to bring about the perfection of the Kingdom of Heaven.

He decided to go for it!

THE TANGLEVILLE CHRISTIAN COALITION MANIFESTO

We, the Christian clergy and laity of Tangleville, hold the following statements to be self-evident:

1. THAT every individual, baptised with the words of the formula, "In the name of the Father, and of the Son and of the Holy Spirit," is a Christian, regardless of the denomination of the Christian clergyperson administering the sacrament.

2. THAT it is the will of God that every baptised Christian live out the mandate of Christ stated in St. Mark's Gospel: *"The first is this, 'Hear, O Israel: the Lord our God, the Lord is one; you shall love the Lord your God with all your heart, and with all your soul, and with all your mind, and with all your strength."*
The second is this, 'You shall love your neighbour as Yourself.'"
(Mark 12:29-31)

3. THAT every Christian refrain from judgement of one another, and of others, to fulfill the commandment of our Lord when He said:

"Do not judge, so that you may not be judged. For with the Judgement you make you will be judged, and the measure you give will be the measure you get." (Matthew 7:1-2)

4. THAT the Christians of Tangleville pledge to work together to:

"Give (render) to the emperor (Caesar) the things that are the emperor's and to God the things that are God's."

(Mark 12:17)

Thereby recognizing and proclaiming that Christianity and secular culture do not by nature walk the same paths nor hold similar values.

5. THAT while affirming the teaching of Christ when He said: *"I am the way, the truth, and the life. No one comes to the Father except through me,"* (John 14:6) nevertheless Christians must tolerate those who choose non-acceptance of the Lord's statement. Christians will refuse to revert to violence against others holding opposing faiths.

6. THAT Christians are free to worship God in various Liturgical styles according to their understanding of Holy Scripture, tradition and reason.

7. THAT where possible, all denominations will strive to support one another in Christian social services to the community, not attempting to duplicate nor compete in such outreach ministries, but to jointly recognize, affirm and

support those parishes and churches where such good work is already being provided to the needy, addicted, abused etc., since each denomination possesses talents and gifts from God and therefore are to be supported in their ministries to the community.

8. THAT remembering the humility of Jesus mandated Him to associate with sinners and pariahs; to wash the feet of His disciples; to visit homes of his theological opponents; and eating with them, that He set the example for how His followers are to actively reach out to the secular world, all the while observing the words of St. Paul who wrote:

   "Do not be conformed to their world, but be transformed by the renewing of your minds, so that you may discern what is the will of God." (Romans 12:2)

9. THAT it is the duty of all Christians to regularly attend worship services and to partake of the Holy Eucharist as celebrated in each particular denomination. Secondly, to support the denomination according to one's financial means, sharing one's talents and spiritual gifts.

10. THAT by the 'stepping out' of active believers, regardless of denominational affiliations, a unified voice of Christ's followers may usher into existence a new dream of Christian unity and the presence of brotherhood and sisterhood thereby challenging secular society's 'anything goes' agenda where religious values are devalued and ignored. For St. Paul wrote: *"We must obey God rather than human authority."* (Acts 5:29)

We, the following hold these statements to be self-evident:

Name: _____   Denomination: _____

Date: _____

Dear fellow clerics: Can you find yourself in a position to sign the above statements? Please read them and get back to me. The Peace of Christ be with you! -Angus.

"Now to wait to hear from the rest of the group," thought Angus. "If it is possible for different denominational leaders to agree to such a manifesto, it will be a miracle in itself!"

CHAPTER SEVENTEEN

DOCTOR McLaughlin had forwarded his draft of the newly requested Tangleville Christian Coalition Manifesto to each of the nine members of the growing interested town clergy. Each had been tasked with reading the document and submitting suggestions for clarity and revisions. It was noted that the document contained ten subsections, obviously patterned after the format of the Ten Commandments given to Moses in the Old Testament.

There was little demand for revision. Some felt that the document was not challenging enough to get the attention of the secular community to whom it would be made public. Others wondered how the term 'stepping out' by the churches could be accomplished. It was obvious that a time-tabled process was needed to do so - well thought out, and clearly articulated to the various parishes, to be understood by the clergy and laity alike. A common prayer was to be drafted to be included in weekly church bulletins for congregational prayers, requesting the will and the power of the Holy Spirit to guide this undertaking.

It was during this Wednesday meeting of the coalition held at the Pentecostal Community Church, hosted by Reverend Jones, that their concerns were about to be tested.

When Reverend Jones had first showed up to join the coalition, nothing was said aloud, but it certainly caused concern amongst some of the gathered all male clergy. For denominations which didn't ordain women, the addition of a female cleric was an anomaly. The first reaction of the Roman Catholic and Orthodox priests was to protest her acceptance. Should they react to include her into the working group?

The two Fathers gave furtive glances towards one another, fully expecting the other to openly protest. Neither did. The draft of the Tangleville Christian Coalition Manifesto to be accepted or modified before them on the agenda contained the words in Item Number 7:

"THAT where possible, all denominations will strive to support one another in Christian social services."

Item Number 6 preceded that objective:

"THAT Christians are free to worship God in various Liturgical styles according to their understanding of Holy Scripture, tradition and reason."

The two realized that if the document was to be approved for publication, it certainly had to pass unanimously by all members of its design team, or otherwise, those who objected would be morally obligated to withdraw their support. If the ecumenical clergy were seen to be divided in its publication, how then could the Christian laity be expected to co-operate? Consequently, their objections to Reverend Jones' acceptance within the coalition were never formally voiced.

The truth was that Reverend Jones herself was initially hesitant to join the working group, the denominational history of Pentecostalism being very different from long established Christian styles of worship.

She was prepared for male rejection, even down right ostracism, by the established clerics of the town. It did not happen! She, after much thought, decided that a united front for a Christian voice in the community was more important than possible humiliation. The risk that her congregation might be left on the outside was too great to take, thus splitting Christ's teaching that "all may be one."

It didn't take long for her fears to be set aside by both parties. For just as the meeting got underway, June, the church secretary, interrupted the gathering to speak to her pastor. She requested her minister to put the meeting on hold and to speak to her in private. The remaining eight clergy, along with Harry Sting, took the opportunity to refill their coffee cups and partake of second helpings of refreshments which had been provided for the meeting. It soon became evident to the male clergy that ministry was no respecter of gender.

Reverend Jones, the host of the meeting, re-entered the room after a ten-minute interlude, her face drawn and pale. She, in halting phrases, began to explain the reason for the interruption of the meeting.

A single mother and her eight-year-old daughter, members of her congregation, had been involved in a terrible car accident last evening on the outskirts of the town. Both had been rushed by helicopter to Tangleville's downtown hospital with third degree burns and were fighting for their lives. Everyone at the table knew of the limited resources for such treatment available in their town's medical facility.

Reverend Jones stated that it was mandatory that the young mother and child would have to be transported to the major burn unit in the big city of St. Magdalene, two hundred miles to the south by helicopter.

Reverend Jones explained that Helen, the single mother, had lost her job as an assembly line worker at a local auto parts plant four months ago, and that her unemployment benefits were to run out in two more weeks. It was a desperate situation for the family. There was no possible way that they could meet their monthly expenses.

Reverend Jones was clearly shaken by the urgency of the news. She set aside the agenda for the meeting for a discussion seeking advice from her peers.

"It seems to me," volunteered Major Huff, "that we have now just been challenged to initiate our first united opportunity to step out together. A Christian mother and daughter are in need. It is our opportunity to put action to the words of our manifesto which we all endorsed."

"I agree," chimed in Father Ivan from St. Nicholas' Parish. "Why don't we establish a fund to assist the family with all of our parishes contributing?"

"If we do," piped up Pastor Richard Head from the non-denominational Community Church, "I recommend that we give it a name - a name associated with scripture, that may include everyone who wishes to give: rich or poor, young or elderly. I don't think that we ought to put a suggested size for the amount of each donation. Just leave it up to the peoples' ability to donate."

It was unanimous to create the fund and to attempt to establish a suitable name for the fund.

Canon Hudson reminded the group of the incident in St. Mark's Gospel where Jesus with His disciples were sitting down opposite the treasury of the temple, watching the crowd putting money into the treasury. The rich were able to donate large sums, but a poor widow came by and put in two small copper coins. Jesus addressed His disciples and said as we read in Saint Mark, Chapter 12, verse 43-44:

"Truly I tell you, this poor widow has put in more than all those who are contributing to the treasury. For all of them have contributed out of their abundance; but she out of her poverty has put in every-thing that she had, all she had to live on."

"The Might of the Mite," declared Father Leo. "There's the name for the fund! Even the youth will be able to contribute. What a learning situation it can be for the children, parents, the financially challenged. I move that becomes our official title for Stepping Out's first initiative."

"All in favor?" requested Reverend Jones. All hands went up. The 'Might of the Mite' officially became a phrase to challenge the Christians of Tangleville.

After the clergy ratified the draft version of Dr. McLaughlin's submission of the Tangleville Christian Coalition Manifesto, and approved it to be submitted to their parishioners, the meeting concluded sharply at two o'clock with Reverend Jones offering a prayer for the healing of the badly burned mother and daughter. The luncheon provided by the Pentecostal volunteers had consisted of chilli, garlic bread, and rice pudding for dessert. Reverend Jones concluded the meeting with the benediction and the little crowd returned to their cars to begin their afternoon parish duties.

Dr. Angus had been instructed to announce the formation of the fundraising event in his next article in the Tangleville Mirror. As Canon Hudson and Father Leo walked together to the parking lot, Matthew asked Leo how he liked the chilli.

"Too mild!" replied Leo.

"Too spicy!" responded Matthew.

They shared a hearty laugh together.

Harry Sting and Dr. McLaughlin remained behind to discuss how they might co-ordinate their two public voices to the community: the radio show and the Cleric Speaks weekly article in the Mirror.

Chapter Eighteen

FOUR weeks had passed since the meeting at Reverend Jones' Pentecostal Church. The slogan, 'The Might of the Mite' had been extremely well received by the laity of all the nine parishes represented by the clergy of the now recognized coalition of clerics. Dr. McLaughlin had introduced the challenge to the Tangleville Christian community in his weekly article in the Mirror. Harry Sting fielded questions by his listening audience during the call-in show, how the name was formulated, relating it to Jesus' words in the New Testament.

As a result, funds began to pour into the non-denominational coffers. No set amount had been suggested as to the size of the individual donations, and no tax receipts were to be given to the donors. The results were far beyond the initial expectations of the planning committee.

Children in the Sunday Schools and the Youth Groups of the various parishes were making their freely given offerings weekly, ranging from a few pennies in some instances to large amounts, money saved up to buy long desired personal belongings: Fitbits, cell phones, the latest fashion in footwear, even earrings and iPads. The meaning of freewill giving was becoming a topic of conversation amongst the Christian community.

A rather unexpected result of the fundraising event within the Christian community was that non-church goers tuned into the Harry Sting Show began to take exception to the growing belief that only the faith communities were capable of charity.

"Why do you have to be a practicing Christian to want to help one's fellow neighbours?" an independent caller challenged Harry during the show. "Altruism is not the sole possession of faith communities. One does not have to be a Christian in order to care for one's neighbour."

Harry could hardly contain himself. He was delighted that he was not on a television show, but rather behind the microphone where his listeners could not detect his grinning face, which would surely give away his old tactics of stirring up his listeners. Of course, 'The Might of the Mite' campaign would not refuse donations from any interested giver, Christian or not! But Harry wanted to convey that the fundraising challenge was the first stage in initiating the stepping out concept for Tangleville's united Christians.

His reply to the angry caller was classic: "God works in mysterious ways, doesn't He? Obviously He is challenging you to love your neighbour as yourself. Yes, indeed, the Churches will be delighted to receive your gift!"

At the end of the show Harry gave the address where anyone could drop off their donation, with Major Huff at the local Salvation Army Citadel acting as steward of the ecumenical fund. Everyone in Tangleville knew where the Citadel was located with its large parking lot. Everyone trusted the Salvation Army when it came to social assistance. So the nine clerics had unanimously agreed that it would be prudent for all their parishes to consolidate their fundraising efforts, with Major Huff in charge. It was another step in adhering to the newly published manifesto which strongly encouraged the non-duplication of Christian outreach.

Within two weeks of the introduction of 'The Might of the Mite' campaign, the nine parishes reported that the fund to assist the non-identified mother and daughter had swelled to slightly over thirty thousand dollars and growing. Christians stepping out together was beginning to register with the Tangleville community. The united front was applauded by the majority of the Christian Church congregations.

When Harry Sting and Dr. McLaughlin remained behind the others following the noon meeting at the Pentecostal Church, they formulated an approach that they were certain would blitz Tangleville with news and plans implementing their newly formulated Christian Manifesto.

They agreed that Dr. Angus would continue to publish his weekly Friday article in the Tangleville Mirror, each publication concentrating on a contentious and controversial issue in secular society. He would convey that he was speaking on behalf of the nine cooperating churches and the following Monday, Harry Sting would then invite clergy to his show to defend the position Dr. Angus had taken the previous Friday.

It was sure to be a winner for Harry, as he knew that many in his listening audience during the call-in segment would be hostile to McLaughlin's previous article in the local newspaper. Ratings were sure to climb, and Harry would be able to revert back to his former times of hosting a show that was controversial. Only this time, he would be able to actually believe in what he was doing: no hypocritical play in motion. Doctor Angus, the erudite scholar and craftsman of prose would be in his element. The combined approach was certain to become the talk of the town!

CHAPTER NINETEEN

DR. Angus was up early and feeling excited. This was his day off from church duties. Normally clerics take Fridays or Mondays as time for relaxation and to be with their spouses since Saturdays are frequently involved with weddings and Sundays are always working days for clergy, often conducting two services during the morning. Dr. Angus usually chose Mondays as time for himself and family. But today, he had reserved the entire morning for writing his weekly submission to the Mirror. As always, the newspaper required his weekly article to be submitted on the Wednesday prior to the Friday publication.

Dr. Angus had checked with the rest of his clerical members of the Tangleville coalition, and it was unanimous. They wanted him to write an article on assisted suicide. He could hardly wait to place the cup of coffee, one cream and no sugar, to the right of his computer, and to begin typing. The words began to flow:

THE CLERIC SPEAKS
by The Rev. Dr. Angus McLaughlin

Dear People of Tangleville:

Today's article is either going to receive your blessings or annoy you to such an extent that you will probably submit a raft of submissions to my email address below. Nonetheless, as a cleric, and a member of the Tangleville Christian Coalition concerned with moral relativism in today's secular society, we feel we must step out and speak out against a movement in today's age which just a few decades ago would be unthinkable: assisted suicide. For Christians of all denominations the concept is an anathema: reprehensible!

Of course, many readers of this article who support such acceptance of choosing to end one's life, will violently and intensely disagree with the church. We expect that they will! And of course in our secular society, devoid of a firm authoritative concept of divine law, one does have the right to do so! After all, in a secular society, lacking allegiance to a sovereign God and the possibility of consequence of judgment after life, anything can and will eventually be acceptable as long as the majority of the population agrees to reject once held sacred and fixed moral obligations as passé. Many will argue: "I am my own master, the captain of my own ship, the god of my own

life. No one has the right to tell me what is right and what is wrong, what is good and what is evil. I will define each issue as I choose!"

The church is not naïve when it comes to dealing with such populist arguments. People of faith do, however, in a free and open society, have the right to state their views. We Christians would argue, that as the stewards of God's fixed eternal laws, we also have the moral obligation to do so! If we didn't do so, secular society would be the first to accuse us of irrelevance and being extraneous voices of the past.

So let me pose a question to both those who oppose assisted suicide and to those who advocate for its acceptance. The question: HOW DOES CHOOSING TO END ONE'S LIFE IMPROVE IT? To this day, I have never been able to discover an acceptable answer to such a philosophical question. The Christian community of course accepts the challenge as being moot. But how does secular society answer it?

There are only two possibilities for moral relativists to do so. The first is to argue that there is nothing beyond physical life as we experience it. That if this life is finite, and this life becomes unbearable, or intolerable, then to exit the unbearable present situation trumps all other matters. Life has a cost! When the price of having life is too high, then cash it in!

This argument makes sense as long as there is no God who holds individuals accountable for actions. Hence, when it comes to accepting the above argument for assisted suicide, then one becomes a gambler, taking the greatest gamble of one's life. If God does not exist, the gambler wins. If God exists, despite one's firmly held convictions that He doesn't then one loses, for one is then held accountable to the judgment of God. Modern secular society appears to be willing to gamble on the possibility of the non-existence of God and His judgment after death. The fact is, one cannot scientifically or philosophically prove that God exists or that He does not. The Christian church has firmly settled the question. The Christian will never gamble on the matter!

The second argument, it seems to me, is the possibility of the following. People say, "If this present life becomes unbearable then ending it will hasten one's entrance to a far superior after life, to some nebulous, undefined spiritual existence." People who believe in reincarnation would be able to rationalize such an existence beyond the present one - perpetually shuffling from one form of existence to another in this world.

Religions that do not hold to Christian accountability on one's actions in this life, and do not predict consequences in the next, could possibly tolerate assisted suicide, perhaps even involuntary euthanasia. But not Christians, who hold firmly to the conviction of a just, Holy God who grants individuals free will while at the same time holding humankind accountable for one's choices in life.

To such aforementioned people, Christians might smugly ask the question: "If God exists and requires accountability of humankind, and if one choses to accept assisted suicide, and then finds oneself committed to hell, can one then choose to commit suicide in hell to end such an existence?" Ridiculous as it sounds to Christians, the question is never asked of modern society exposing moral relativism. Perhaps it should be posed!

Secular society considers 'assisted' suicide as progressive legislation, but Christians consider it 'spiritual' suicide. Thus Christians have no choice but to reject the concept in its entirety, yet acknowledging that in an open democratic society, moral relativism for many trumps God given moral absolutes. That's why Christians are required to step out, refusing to endorse such so called tolerant attitudes. Christians know 'how to' answer the question, how does choosing to end one's life improve it? It can't! But Christians are waiting for the moral relativists to do so!

We, the Christian Coalition, look forward to your response to this article.

All responses to this article can reach me by email to try to give a rational rebuttal.

drangus@fastmail.com.

Chapter Twenty

In preparation for his Monday morning show, Harry had decided to ask the Rev. Dieter Muller from St. Peter's Lutheran parish and Pastor Richard Head from the non-denominational Community Church to be his guests for the day. Both had eagerly agreed to do so, and were well aware that they would be fielding questions from Sting's call-in audience.

Harry had decided to change the format of the first section of the show to become a guest/call-in format. In the past the first segment was normally an interview time with his guests, while the second portion was the listener's time to participate. Harry knew that his audience would be chomping at the bit to respond to Dr. McLaughlin's previously published 'The Cleric Speaks' in the Tangleville Mirror. It was certain to be the talk of the town!

Rev. Muller, Pastor Richard and Harry had agreed that they would meet in AM KNOW's offices a full thirty minutes prior to the show to plan how they would handle the call-in audience. They agreed that, as the host, Harry would appear to be the neutral moderator, fielding questions from the audience to his two clerical guests. What the audience would not know or see was how each responder to difficult questions would be selected by Harry. All each had to do to signal Harry was to simply raise a hand to tell him that one was eager and pleased to do so. If the other clergy person wished to pick up and expand on what the first responder had said, Harry would signal to allow that person to continue to answer the caller. The beauty of radio is that the audience can only hear voices, not the antics of the crew behind the microphones.

At precisely 10:05, Harry's professional voice took over from the hourly newsreader:

> "Good morning and welcome dear listeners of Tangleville. You will find the format of this one hour show slightly altered for today. As you know, my first half hour is always an interview time with my guests. The second half hour is your time to call in and to respond to what you have heard. But this morning the entire hour is yours! So stand by your telephone, for the lines are likely to be jammed this morning. That is because my guests are The Reverend Dieter Muller, the Lutheran cleric, from St. Peter's Lutheran Church and Pastor Richard Head from the non-denominational Community Church, both from downtown Tangleville. They are members of the newly formed Tangleville Community Coalition of Clerics here in our town and signing members of the Manifesto that was recently published last Friday in the Tangleville Mirror. I know that you, as astute listeners, will want to challenge these two clerics on what they have signed. Do you agree with Dr. Angus McLaughlin's article which he recently published, or not?" Harry winked

at his two guests, a wide grin on his face. "Now is your opportunity to speak your mind!"

The five phone lines to the show immediately flashed red. Before Harry took the first call he whispered to his guests, "I think this is going to be a minefield. Enjoy!"

The prompter in front of Harry indicated that the caller was Mary, a first-time caller, who appeared angry with the clergy of Tangleville.

"Good morning Mary, and welcome to the show! What have you got to say to my guests this morning?"

"Harry, I'm so angry that I could spit! It is a good thing that I'm not there in your broadcast booth, or I'd do so on your two guests today!"

"Why Mary? What has got you so riled?"

"Harry, what gives the clergy the right to tell me what I can or can't do with my own body?"

"Mary, let's be a bit clearer. What specifically are you referring to when you say the words 'my own body?'"

"The right to end my life if I so choose. If life became so intolerable that I can't take it any longer, then it is my choice to do so. Not anyone else's and especially not the clergy to tell me not to do so."

"I'm going to turn you over to one of my guests, okay? Which one of you wishes to respond to Mary?"

"I don't care," the caller piped up. "All clergy are the same!"

Harry was all smiles as he waited for one of his guests to raise a hand. Rev. Muller was eager to respond.

"Mary, this is Rev. Muller. You have asked a question that the church has heard before: many times, in fact. But let me ask you a question. Is your life really your life?"

"Of course it is," snapped Mary.

"Let me ask you Mary, did you give life to yourself or was it passed on to you at the time of your birth by your parents?"

"That's a silly question. Of course I was given birth. You know that."

"So life is then a gift! Are you accustomed to tossing gifts back to those who in love gave you the gift?"

"My parents are dead, so your question is non-debatable, a moot argument."

"Do you have any offspring? Close friends? People who love you and will miss you if you choose to cease to exist?"

"Yes, of course. We all do! What has that got to do with my personal autonomy?"

"Life is not cheap! It is not for sale! It is not ours alone! We all have an interest in the lives of one another - especially God, the Creator, the giver of life. How do you think God feels when you throw your life back into His face? Even His Son, Jesus Christ, refused to do that! He suffered on the cross because suffering was part of God's plan for the redemption of the world, through the life of Christ, as the supreme sacrifice for sin. Christ could have refused to be nailed to the cross. But He didn't! Are you willing to tell us that our Lord's suffering has no meaning?"

"I don't believe in a creator! Don't use that God talk with me!"

"Ah, the truth is out. You're a gambler! You are gambling that God does not exist and therefore you are unaccountable to the supreme giver of life. Prove to us that there is no God!"

"You know I can't do that," she retorted.

"If God does exist and He holds us accountable for our choices in life, and if He didn't spare the suffering of His own Son, do you not think that a finite time of suffering in this world is a far better bet than the possibility of suffering for eternity in hell?

The Church, you see, believes that God does exist, and we Christians believe that even suffering has meant the Church does not debate free will. In your case, the right to choose assisted suicide - you do have that choice! What we argue is that if God exists, it is foolish to reject the will of God. It is called the way of the Cross, following in the footsteps of Christ!"

"I'm willing to take that gamble!" Mary snapped.

"And you have the right to do so. In turn, however, the church has the right to beg to differ in the making of such choices. Surely you, a proponent of free will would not deny those who disagree with your conclusions to proclaim opposite views!"

"Fair enough, I concede your point. But I'm not changing my mind!"

Pastor Head appeared to relish the opportunity to join in to the conversation.

"Mary," he chimed in, "how would you respond to the question that if modern medicine - perhaps not yet, but in the near future - could be able to thoroughly control pain during one's final days before death? Would you be willing to acknowledge that that might be superior to ending one's life? To let natural death occur, while being rendered pain free in the process? After all, the hospice movement is making great strides in this area."

"But what if I can't do anything for myself as I await death? Can't feed myself, can't control bodily functions, can't speak, can't communicate with friends and family?"

"Were you not in that same situation a long time ago - the first year or so of your life? Were we not all totally helpless, totally dependent on others at the time of our birth? Love supplied your early needs. Love will always be there during our final days. Love is God's gift to humanity! Love is freely given, and we in turn freely dispense love. That is the message of Christianity. Have you never heard of the old adage 'We are all once an adult and twice a child?'"

"Harry, I'm not taking this any longer." And with that, Mary slammed down the receiver and hung up on the show.

Rev Muller broke the silence, "Mr. Sting, we all have the right to gamble with difficult choices in life in this world. But if God exists, the stakes of doing so determine one's eternal existence. The church does not bet against God!"

The lines were jammed with people waiting to get on the air. Harry took the next caller who was fully in agreement with Dr. McLaughlin's article in the Mirror and who said so to Rev. Muller and Pastor Richard. Harry was keeping a running tally of the positions his audience was registering, those for and those against doctor-assisted suicide. The callers seemed to be about equally divided in their responses, with those who were against such a position of choosing assistance to end one's life indicating that they were regular church attendees, and those for the concept either tended to be agnostics, atheists, or lapsed religious observers.

It was a highly emotional hour. People expressed their positions passionately, and there appeared to be no middle ground in their minds. As far as the success of the program was concerned, Harry was delighted. His ratings were sure to be acknowledged by the station managers.

However, as much as Harry appeared on the show to be a neutral mediator both he and his two guests knew where, from a theological perspective, he stood on the matter. Harry knew that it was the perfect opportunity for his guests to offer explanations as to why people would be willing to choose to end life rather than to live with the consequences of doing so.

As caller after caller was interviewed, the following explanations for not choosing assisted death were offered by the two clergy guests:

Rev Muller, ever the academic, who had read extensively on such matters noted that almost all who actually commit suicide have some sort of mental health issues, such as schizophrenia, bipolar disorder, and alcohol and drug addiction among others. He had discovered through research that up to 93-94% of those commit the act without doctor assistance. He emphasized that such disorders are treatable and so suicide is unmerited for people with such disorders.

Pastor Head noted that those requesting suicide are often ambivalent, often really making an attempt for a cry for help, to test for another person's coming to offer care and affection, and to express a fear of abandonment. Suicide is escapism from reality and frustration, aggression turned inward. He noted that psychiatrists have long suggested that underlying a suicidal person's wish to end his life is actually a wish to be rescued.

Both guests agreed that in secular society, many do not wish to acknowledge that they are accountable to the authority of a God who will hold them responsible for actions taken during our earthly life. Such people want to be their own god, accountable only to one's self and the current enforceable laws of secularism.

In the last minutes of the show, Harry offered each of his guests the opportunity to sum up their reactions to the morning program. Both were ready and eager to do so.

Rev Muller was adamant in conveying to the audience that, "Christianity, especially the Tangleville Christian Coalition, never advocates or relies upon force in conveying the Good News to unbelievers. Rather, Christians are taught to lead by example, by peaceful co-existence with the secular world. Love of neighbour should be extended to everyone, regardless of religious convictions or lack thereof. When Christians disagree with the morals and lifestyles of modern society, judgment of such conduct is best left to the will of God, not to Christians themselves who are mandated to reach out to all. Hence all who disagree with the teachings of Christianity are not in any way to feel threatened. Everyone has the right to agree or disagree with the Church. Likewise, the Church has the right to express and convey its message to non-believers. God bless you all!"

Pastor Head picked up where Rev Muller ended by saying, "The Tangleville Christian Manifesto ends with the Biblical statement, 'We must obey God rather than human authority' from Acts 5:29. That is why believers are admonished to step out from being drafted into contemporary activities that violate their consciences. Stepping out is the least violent and most peaceful way of saying, 'We do not wish to participate in that which we feel is profane.' In a free and open society, everyone has the right to non-participation in matters of life which cause concern for peace of mind. Can anyone honestly criticize the Church for advocating such actions of its members?"

Harry ended the show, grinning across at his guests. "Thank-you Pastor Head and Rev Muller for being my guests today! To you, my listeners, I wish to convey my appreciation for taking the time to call in and participate in today's show. Perhaps you have been influenced by what we were challenged to consider by my guests. I will invite other members of the Christian Coalition to be future guests on my show to give us their views on divisive topics of the day. You will not want to miss their thoughtful and perhaps thought-provoking opinions. Until next broadcast, blessings!"

When the On Air sign went out, Rev Muller reminded Harry that the term 'blessings' conveyed religious meaning.

"I know," replied Harry. "Let's see if the audience caught it!"

Chapter Twenty-One

HARRY was energized; his show's ratings were skyrocketing. Tangleville once again was listening and definitely aroused!

It was a team effort with Dr. McLaughlin's Friday submission of 'The Cleric Speaks' to the Tangleville Mirror, just in time for the weekend publication to a divided religious community, and then on Monday, Harry would exploit the two or more sides of the controversy generated by McLaughlin's official voice of the coalition of churches.

It was a brilliant, co-operative partnership. As far as the listening public was concerned, Harry was still considered a neutral mediator for the call-in guests on the show. The two weekly invited clergy guests each Monday were officially expected to represent the views and positions of the formally published Christian Manifesto. The call-in guests were permitted to agree or disagree with the clergy on each show. But Harry was having a difficult time trying to come across as the detached host, for clearly it was becoming quite obvious to some of his audience that he really was sympathetic to views of the religious positions projected in Dr. McLaughlin's articles. This was beginning to infuriate anti-religious secularists who were violently opposed to what they considered religious interventionists.

* * *

Annie and Harry were enjoying a mid-Sunday afternoon drive in her 1972 Jaguar XKE convertible, top down. Annie was behind the wheel when Harry asked the question, "What can I do to somehow let the clergy of the community know how grateful I am to be part of their stepping out plans for Tangleville? They are professional clergy and I can't help but feel how fortunate I am to be a small cog in their growing influence in town. I'm not theologically trained as they are, yet they accept me as an equal in their meetings. Because of them, my show is thriving. Any suggestions on how I should show my gratitude?"

Annie was completely at ease behind the wheel, shifting effortlessly through the gears of the four speed manual transmission. The Jag and she functioned as a unit, drifting through corners with the ease of a professional driver.

"Why does it have to be only you?" she asked. "Haven't we always been a team in our marriage? What's wrong with both of us saying thanks?"

She was Annie at her best: lover, critic, helpmate, accomplished artist, not only with paint on canvas, but as the brilliant marriage partner who was always able to keep Harry firmly grounded in reality. To Harry and their closest friends, she was just Annie. To her many admiring and adoring art fans, she was A.F. Antonov, Anastasia, the world-renowned professional artist. Over the years she had become recognized as a major force in the art world. She was widely sought after as an art critic, and had become independently wealthy over the years. Harry knew how fortunate he was to have married this exceptional woman.

"What are you getting at, Annie?" asked Harry. "I'm missing out on something, aren't I ?"

"You've had the privilege of meeting and working with the clergy of Tangleville," she replied. "The only ones I know are Canon Hudson and Fr. Fedosov, my priest. I'd like to get to know the others and especially their secretaries and office staff, their spouses - why not get everyone together over a meal and let us all socialize. Let's host an evening dinner party at one of Tangleville's top restaurants, invite all the clergy and their better halves and the office staff of each of the parishes and have a night of mingling and getting to know each other. We can together say our thank-yous to the Tangleville Christian Coalition. I'll bet it's only the clergy who know one another. We spouses need to do likewise!"

"Annie, brilliant! Will you handle the details? You are much better at these things than I am!"

"Harry, don't pull that old soft-soap routine on me. I know your ways. But yes, I'll handle it! You simply supply me with a list of the parishes, the names of the clergy and get the mailing addresses of everyone involved, and I'll take care of it. Let's make it an easy night for everyone - not a formal affair, just smart casual dress. And let's make it known there are to be no thank-you gifts to be brought to the restaurant. It will be our act of gratitude to the parish communities!"

Annie expertly pulled the Jag into a hairpin curve on one of Tangleville's back roads. She was a most competent lady in so many ways. Harry knew that he was the most fortunate individual in Tangleville to have her as his wife! He wouldn't admit to many people, but he had often wondered to himself what she ever saw in him when she'd said "I do" before the altar on the day of their marriage.

They stopped for an ice cream cone on the way back to their upscale home on Upper Manhattan Crescent. Annie was driving with one hand on the wheel, the other on the four speed stick shift lever, speeding a little faster than usual. It was obvious that she wanted to get to her Mac to begin the design of an invitation to be used to invite guests. Harry, in the passenger bucket seat, was still finishing off the last bites of his blueberry cone as they pulled into the driveway.

"Put the coffee on! I've got work to do," Annie instructed her spouse as she headed to her study. Within fifteen minutes, she'd produced a draft invitation:

You're Invited

To a

Stepping Out Dinner Party

hosted by

Harry & Anastasia Sting

June 18, 2016

at

The Surf 'n Turf Restaurant

5438 Memory Lane

Tangleville

Dress: Smart Casual   No gifts to the hosts

R.S.V.P. to Annie by June 10th

555-918-1234 or

afantonov@fastmail.com

"What do you think?" Annie asked as she presented Harry with the first draft.

"Couldn't have done it better myself!" he told her as he gave her a kiss on the cheek. Ever the feisty, coy Annie, she gave her husband a right-fisted smack on his jaw - light enough to barely injure a mosquito. Harry inwardly smiled.

CHAPTER TWENTY-TWO

THE nine clerical members had last met two weeks ago at The Rev. Dieter Muller's Lutheran Church. To their delight, three more influential clergy arrived unannounced for the meeting and requested membership in the coalition, which now totalled a dozen members.

The new members included: The Rev. Jim Adams, rector of St. Timothy's, the other Anglican downtown Tangleville parish; Father Thomas McCann, rector of St. Joseph's Roman Catholic parish in the suburbs of the town; and The Rev. James Johnson, minister of the African Methodist Episcopal congregation located in the middle of Tangleville.

"Looks like we now have a membership of twelve disciples," quipped Dr. Angus. "What could be more appropriate than twelve ordained clergy cooperating to follow their Lord?"

Harry, in his usual inquisitive way, asked, "What are you going to do with me? I'm not ordained."

"Ah, you are the first of the beginning of the so-called 'seventy' Jesus sent out as frontmen to announce His presence in His three-year ministry. All you need to do now is to add sixty-nine more to your membership! Think you can do it?" teased Rev. James.

"Well, you may be surprised," retorted Harry. "Remember, I've got far more folks in the pews than any of you! My pulpit is a radio mic!"

The group agreed it was a very successful meeting. They unanimously encouraged Dr. Angus to continue to write his weekly article for the Tangleville Mirror, and suggested topics for him to cover in future editions: Sunday shopping, their objection to secular society's scheduling of sports events that coincided with Sunday morning worship times, secular religion, and moral relativism. They pledged that if Dr. Angus needed more suggestions for future articles, that they would be quite able to supply him with additional topics for publication.

As expected, everyone applauded Harry for his role in following up on Mondays with his interviews using two of the coalition's disciples as guests. Harry was given the freedom to choose from the twelve whomever he wished to fill the guest seats for the two thirty-minute segments on AM KNOW. He was amazed at the willingness of the group to volunteer to sit before his often antagonistic audience. Clearly, the clergy of Tangleville were taking their mandate to step out for unity very seriously.

* * *

The June 18th Stepping Out Dinner Party at the Surf 'n Turf Restaurant was a phenomenal evening – everyone said so. A total of fifty-three invited guests arrived for the gathering which included all the members of the clergy, their spouses, and support staff of the twelve congregations. Annie and Harry greeted each guest at the entrance of the reserved dining room area, giving out name tags to be worn for the evening. The clergy already knew each other, but the spouses, of course, did not. It didn't take long for the spouses to begin mingling even before sitting down for the first course to be served. It was evident that there was real interest in learning about one another's families and whether or not the spouses were employed in professions other than being a cleric's partner. As well, they discussed their roles as clergy spouses.

But it was the support staff that really hit it off - comparing notes on their parish responsibilities, the office equipment that was available for them in their places of employment, their hours of work, even the amount of vacation time that was part of their contracts.

It was difficult for Harry and Annie following the pre-dinner reception to finally steer everyone to be seated for the meal. The support staff made it clear that they wished to be seated next to one another. Annie was pleased to see that there was genuine enthusiasm right from the beginning of the evening. All her planning for the event was obviously paying off. Annie, in high heels, was attired in a simple black dress with a single strand of pearls to compliment her good taste. She told Harry he looked splendid in his grey dress slacks, blue navy blazer and an open neck dress shirt. They were a picture of class and civility.

Annie and Harry stood at the head table, side by side, but it was Annie who warmly welcomed their guests, ever the gracious and accomplished lady.

After the brief greeting, she called upon Fr. Ivan Fedosov, her parish priest, to give the blessing for the meal about to be served. With everyone standing, Fr. Ivan recited a prayer - first in Russian, and then in English. Everyone concluded with an amen, the Romans, the Anglicans and the Orthodox crossing themselves when Fr. Ivan proclaimed the words, "In the name of the Father, and the Son, and the Holy Spirit."

The choices for the main entree were roast beef and a baked potato with a choice of vegetables, or an assortment of seafood: three kinds of shrimp, crab legs, several varieties of fish, or lobster. The two sides were white rice and cauliflower. Dessert was either ice cream with one of several toppings, chocolate brownies, and apple or blueberry pie. Coffee and tea were available throughout the entire meal.

Canon Matthew had just ordered lobster, his favourite seafood, when his cellphone rang. Excusing himself from the table, he walked out into the lobby to answer the call. It was a nurse calling from Tangleville's Downtown Community Hospital.

"Canon Hudson, we have an urgent request for you to come immediately to room 3462. The husband of Audrey Holmes, Jack, is possibly near death. Mrs. Holmes wants you to come and be at his bedside. Can you come?"

"I'll be there in fifteen minutes. Tell Audrey that I am on my way. And tell her that I'll hold both of them in my prayers!"

Canon Matthew hurriedly returned to the dinner setting and approached Annie and Harry at the head table. Whispering in their ears, he explained the situation and excused himself from the gathering.

"Tell the rest of the folk at an appropriate time why I have to leave. I'm going to let Maggie know - she will understand. Please remind her to be sure and bring the lobster I ordered home to be my dinner later on!"

Canon Hudson, as quietly as he could, left the room after speaking briefly with Maggie. She said that she would get a ride home with Fr. Jim Adams and his wife Jackie following the evening event, as she expected that he would likely be late in getting home from the hospital.

It took Canon Hudson exactly twelve minutes to make it from the Surf 'n Turf Restaurant to the parking lot of the hospital. He rushed to the third floor to 3462, a private room, where he found Audrey waiting for him to arrive, sitting in a chair next to Jack's bed, holding his hand.

Audrey, a faithful member of the parish quickly rose from the chair, rushed over to Canon Matthew, threw her arms around him and quickly led him into the hallway, out of hearing of her husband. In the hallway she explained:

"Canon, Jack has been diagnosed with an inoperable aneurysm in the brain. The doctors tell us it is only a matter of time until it ruptures. You know that he has never attended church with me. He always claimed that he was an agnostic, that he couldn't get his head around the possible existence of an all-powerful God. He can't recall whether he had ever been baptized as a child, and here is the good news: he wants to come to grips with dying, and before he dies, he wants to claim Jesus Christ as Lord of his life. That is why I called for you. I know that he is utterly serious in committing his life to Christ!"

A tear was slowly running down both cheeks as she waited for Canon Hudson to reply.

"Audrey, this is an answer to our prayers. Does he know that I'm coming tonight?"

"Yes! In fact, he demanded that I call you at this late hour."

"Okay, Audrey. We are going to go into his room together. You tell him that I've arrived, and invite him to inform me what he has already told you about his desire to be certain of his baptism." They entered the room.

"Jack, Canon Hudson is here. I know that you are glad to see him. Let me raise up your bed to a seating position so that you two can talk. I'm going to go down to the cafeteria to get a bite to eat. I've not eaten since seven o'clock this morning. You two can talk while I'm away.

You know what you and I talked about before you asked me to call Father Hudson".."

Audrey with her hand in her husband's hand, smiled at Canon Hudson as she made that excuse to leave her husband's room, thereby permitting Jack and Canon Hudson to be alone for a time of private conversation.

Canon Hudson soon learned that Jack was troubled. It only took a few minutes for Jack to get the niceties of polite conversation set aside before he turned the conversation over to what was the real reason for his request for a clergy visit.

"Canon, you know that I've never pretended to be a religious person. I'm sure that Audrey has told you that I've always, since the early days of our marriage, derided and mocked her insistence upon reading her Bible, her regular prayer life, and her faithful attendance at St. Bart's. But she never condemned me in return. She is a model of Christian virtue! She has never told me so, but I know that she has been praying for me to come to faith in Jesus Christ."

Canon Hudson moved a little closer to the bedside to observe Jack's demeanor as he began to wrestle with his distraught conscience.

"Go on Jack, I'm listening."

Jack needed to be heard - this was as close to a confession as he had ever made in his life. It was important that he should eventually verbalize what he felt, that he needed to turn around his misgivings of not living a life of spiritual discipleship.

Finally, Canon Hudson was willing to challenge Jack:

"What do you propose to do about your life? Are you telling me that because of your serious medical condition that you've reached the point of conviction? Are you having a spiritual crisis because you are afraid to die? Be honest! Is it fear of death that has motivated you to talk to me?"

"Yes, Canon. I'm afraid to die without first obtaining spiritual peace with God. I've been wrestling with matters of the soul for some time now. But the doctor's diagnosis of probable sudden death has settled the matter. I can't wait any longer to make my confession of sins. That's why I called for you. I'm not even sure that I was baptised as a child. My parents never told me that they had me 'done,' as so many of my former anti-religious friends would put it!"

Canon Hudson reached across the bed and grasped the other man's hand.

"Jack, you need to undergo and complete two sacred observances. You need to be baptised. Since you don't know whether or not you were baptised as an infant, I will conduct what is known in Anglicanism as a 'conditional baptism.' I will use the words that say, 'If you are not already baptised, Jack, I baptise you…'

Is it your desire to confess Jesus Christ as Lord and Savior?"

Tears were welling up in Jack's eyes. He reached for a fistful of tissues as he tried to dry his cheeks and compose his demeanor. Canon Hudson knew that Jack was ready to begin a new life in Christ.

"We we are alone in this room," Canon Hudson told him. "I will tell the nursing staff not to interrupt us for the next twenty minutes while you make your confession. Then we will call for Audrey and I will baptise you immediately following her arrival. Are you ready?"

"Absolutely! Tell me what I have to do," Jack replied.

Canon Hudson always carried a copy of the Prayer Book with him. Opening the book, he turned to the prayer of a penitent.

"Jack, read this prayer of confession before God and myself. When you come to the word 'especially,' the time for you to confess personal sins, list them one by one. Take as much time as you need, and then continue with the printed Prayer Book words."

Jack, in a clear and confident voice began to read the words of a penitent: *"Most merciful God, have mercy on me. In your compassion forgive my sins, both known and unknown, things done and left undone, especially…"* He continued, listing his sins one by one, taking a full eight minutes. Then he read again from the prayer book, *""O God, uphold me by your Spirit that I may live and serve you in newness of life, for the honour and glory of your name; through Jesus Christ our Lord. Amen."*

After they together recited the Lord's Prayer, Canon Matthew gave Jack absolution, the assurance that his sins were forgiven by God, and they embraced and wept together, taking a good five minutes to regain their composure..

There was a knock at the door. It was Audrey carrying three cups of coffee.

"Your timing is perfect," Canon Hudson told her. Jack wants me to baptise him right here in his room. He has just made his peace with God. Now he wants to be baptised. Go and get me a small container of water. This is the day of new birth for Jack!"

While Audrey was getting water and a fresh clean towel, two nurses walked into Jack's room. They were informed of the impending baptism of their patient, and both being faithful Christians, one a Baptist and the other a Roman Catholic, asked if they could be present for the holy sacrament. With Audrey holding Jack's hand and the two nurses holding each other's hand, Canon Hudson, three times pouring copious handfuls of water over the head of Jack, said those ancient sacred words:

"If you are not already baptised, Jack, I baptise you in the name of the Father and of the Son and of the Holy Spirit. Amen."

Water was everywhere, as the three handfuls of liquid ran down onto Jack's pajamas and the bed sheets, one handful after the word 'Father,' the second after the word 'Son,' and the third at the time of the words 'Holy Spirit.' The two nurses rushed to happily dry off the wet sheets and to congratulate their patient.

Outside of the day Audrey made her wedding vows to Jack decades before, she told him, it was one of the happiest days of her life. Her prayers had been answered!

At 11:30, Canon Hudson took his leave. The outside light was on when he arrived home, but he knew that Maggie would long ago have returned from the Surf 'n Turf dinner.

There was only one task Canon Matthew needed to accomplish downstairs before turning in for the night - to check the refrigerator to see if his uneaten lobster was there. It was!

CHAPTER TWENTY-THREE

THERE comes a time in most peoples' lives, sometimes in early middle age, when most individuals pause to take inventory of their past. Questions arise such as, "What have I accomplished in life? Where am I going? What is still left on my bucket list, so to speak? If I should die tomorrow, what is it that I should have attempted to do, at least tried to explore, and didn't?"

Harry Sting was at the stage in life where he had accomplished far more than most of his friends and acquaintances. He was an example of a type-A personality, seldom taking time to smell the roses, to view a beautiful sunset, to think about what he might still wish to explore in the future.

On one Monday afternoon in his office at the Samaritan Inn, following another successful morning radio show, he was in an unusually pensive mood. He told the receptionist to hold all of his calls for the next hour. His timetable was clear for the entire afternoon. The agenda for the next Board of Directors' meeting was completed and in the hands of his secretary. His thoughts turned to the past years of his existence.

Being the organized and rational person he had become, he began to jot down, in no particular order, the highlights and accomplishments of his life. He would, he mused, put them in chronological order at a later date.

He thought back to how fortunate he had been in growing up in a home where both parents were disciplinarians with high expectations for him. He never questioned their love for each other and especially for himself. They were morally good people as society would judge them, but not religious in any formal fashion. They considered going to church a waste of a Sunday morning - religion was for the weak and the needy, a crutch for those who could not face the realities of life. Harry, during his university years, only had his inherited conviction of religion's role reinforced. Religion could be exploited, and he willingly had been the one to do so. That's why, he in his early years in radio railed against religious observers.

His marriage to Annie was one of the best things that ever had happened to him. She was the perfect partner: bright, extremely talented, loving, and she tolerated him when he made fun of her religious convictions. Whenever their conversations turned to his disdain for Christian faith, she would smile that coy smile of hers and simply say, "I'll pray for you!"

Money, it turned out, was not to be an issue in his life. Annie, because of her artistic talents, had become a multi-millionaire. He, as a result, knew that he could dabble in playing the rabble-rousing host at AM KNOW with its low salary. If they decided to fire him from his post, so be it! The Stings would never miss his meagre income.

He couldn't explain it at the time, but everything had changed that morning a few years ago when the Rev.Canon Dr. Barclay Steadmore, the former rector of St. Bartholomew's Anglican Church downtown, arrived as his morning clerical guest on his show. Steadmore was just to have been another bit of human clerical fodder for his first half-hour of the show, to be exploited to keep up his ratings with the secular listening audience. He knew that he would never forget how Steadmore didn't show up wearing his clerical collar, and had tricked him by asking, "Do you want me to answer your questions today as an individual wearing my sacred hat as a theologian, or do you want me to respond wearing my secular hat, the way that society would answer your questions?" The truth was, that he, as a non-religious individual, really didn't quite understand what Dr. Steadmore meant. He had replied, "Well, you're not wearing your collar. Answer wearing your secular hat."

That question by Steadmore was the beginning of his slowly developing interest in Christianity. Annie's prayers were at the incubation stage of being answered!

There followed the unexpected developing friendship between Steadmore and himself and that of Annie, his spouse and Faith, Steadmore's wife. Both he and Steadmore began to wrestle with the hypocrisy of their times together on subsequent shows – he, pretending to detest Steadmore's religious arguments, and Dr. Steadmore fighting against his newly found popularity in the community whenever he managed to best Harry. Both were really playing a game and although it was advantageous to continue to do so, each began to detect a pebble in their shoe, so to speak: a pricking of conscience that could not continue or be ignored.

He remembered so clearly the time of his confession before Dr. Steadmore, that occasion in his downstairs office. He and Annie were hosting a late evening dinner with Barclay and Faith. After the meal, he had invited Barclay to join him downstairs on the pretense of wanting to show his guest some of Annie's works of art. During that time he finally got around to the real reason that the Steadmores were invited: his struggling with conscience, his recent unexplainable feelings of a need for a relationship with God. The result was that he made his confession before Dr. Steadmore and his friend, the priest, gave him absolution. He'd wept tears of relief and joy all mixed in with an unexplainable feeling of new found freedom of being. Events took place in short order which included his baptism and confirmation with membership at St. Bart's parish.

He became the director of the Samaritan Inn, Tangleville's domestic violence shelter, now open with a new separate building for males dealing with addictions. The complex was now in the process of expansion because of his leadership abilities. His radio show was altered to become, not an hour of controversy, but a new educational format where experts were invited as guests to discuss such topics as medicine, environmentalism, public safety, healthy lifestyles, exercise and nutrition. He was aware that his public image was being taken seriously by the majority of his new listening audience.

Two of the most valued honours he cherished were when Bishop Strictman conferred upon him the title of 'Lay Canon' and subsequently invited him to become the Communications Director for the Diocese of New Avondale. As a result, he was now involved with confidential matters to which only his bishop and the diocesan lawyers were privy. He was entrusted with dealing with the secular media whenever such matters were revealed or leaked to the press. "What a one hundred and eighty degree turn for me", he thought. "Before I revelled in gossip and mischief over the air. Now I'm protecting the good name of the church"!

There was one matter which truly warmed his heart: he and Annie working together for church unity on the Stepping Out agenda, which was quickly becoming a positive movement for Christianity in Tangleville -- recognizing that it was after Annie and he hosted the Stepping Out dinner party that it really became obvious that the future of the movement for Christian unity was to lie with the laity. Soon after meeting at the dinner party, the staff members of the parishes had organized to gather on a semi-monthly basis: once in each other's churches, and once at a suitable restaurant downtown. They were taking over as the voices for Christian unity in a fashion that the clerics could never do. The clerics were expected to preach, teach, celebrate the sacraments, conduct weddings and funerals, visit the sick - but it was the laity who were everyday amongst the people, putting theological theory into practice, demonstrating the universal message of the Good News in the workplaces, the supermarkets, the home, the neighborhoods. Clerics are considered as professional Christians, expected to 'talk the talk,' but it is the laity who 'walk the walk' in the real world of rubbing shoulders with the rest of humanity.

It was becoming increasingly clear to himself that as a lay person, his role was to work with the Christian communities in a fashion that the twelve clerics could never quite do. God had placed him in two camps: a valuable lay associate member with the ordained coalition, and the radio spokesman for the vast numbers of lay believers in the town, with Annie as his silent partner.

"How could he, before his conversion, ever have imagined that God had a unique plan for his life? But that is another example of the mystery of how God intervenes in the affairs of humanity. He did so with Abraham, Moses, and St. Paul", he mused. "Why should a modern day Christian be surprised when God calls His followers to leadership? I wonder what is next that God has in store for Annie and me"?

The sound of the ringing of his cell phone interrupted his reflection. Since Harry had given his cell number to only a select group of people, he felt compelled to answer it.

"Harry, it's Angus over at St. Andrew's. That receptionist of yours is very protective of you. I couldn't get past her. What are you doing?"

"Doctor, she's not looking for a new position so don't even think of attempting to entice her to go over and work for you Presbyterians! What's up?"

"A couple of exciting things! I want to give you the heads up that my article in the Mirror this coming Friday will deal with secular religion. You may want to deal with the topic on your Monday show."

"Great, Doctor. I'll be pleased to deal with the fallout of your article." Harry grinned as he teased Angus.

"And here's the other good news, Harry. I've learned that the combined staff of the twelve churches in town are planning for a community church picnic on the last Saturday of the month. It will be open to all the people of the congregations, along with anyone from the town who wishes to join in. Can you promote it over your shows?"

"I'll bet that Annie already knows of this gathering. I'm going to go home and accuse her of withholding information," chuckled Harry. "Of course, I'll be happy to do my part. By the way, how is your golf handicap these days?"

"Let's not go there, Harry. All I will say is that it's lower than yours!"

It was a great day, mused Harry as he drove home to dinner in his recently-purchased Audi SUV. God is a God of surprises!

CHAPTER TWENTY-FOUR

DR. Angus was mentally preparing to write his upcoming Friday publication in the Tangleville Mirror. He had decided on the gist of the article – as he had informed Harry, it would involve secularism, focusing and narrowed down to secular religion in its applications to modern culture.

Angus knew that it would be a difficult topic to deal with. He was aware that there were positive aspects of secularism, but at the same time many elements of the movement competed and conflicted with Christian practice. How to be fair in this submission to the local news-paper was going to be a challenge - especially when hard core positions are taken by non-religious new agers, atheists, and agnostics. But Dr. Angus was never known to shy away from anything controversial.

THE CLERIC SPEAKS

by The Rev. Dr. Angus McLaughlin

Dear People of Tangleville:

What is a Christian to do? Indeed, how is anyone who pos-sesses spiritual convictions going to co-exist with the secular culture in which we presently collide? This question is a fundamental problem for people of faith - especially as secularism increasingly becomes the norm in our age.

But first, what is 'secularism?' Does it have merits in a pluralistic society? Is everything that secularism promotes contrary to Christian values?

Secularism draws its intellectual roots from Greek and Roman philosophers such as Epicurus and Marcus Aurelius and from Enlightenment thinkers such as John Locke, Voltaire, Baruch Spinoza, Thomas Jefferson and Thomas Paine. More up to date recent thinkers include Robert Ingersol and Bertrand Russell.

But it was Jacob Holyoake, an agnostic, who invented the term 'secularism' in 1851. The positive aspects of secularism are commendable in an open and democratic society. These include:

1) Deep respect for individuals and the small groups of which they are a part;

2) Equality before the law for all people;

3) Each individual should be helped to realize one's particular gifts;

4) Breaking down the barriers of class and caste; and

5) The understanding that there is light and guidance in discovered truth outside of the principles of sacred truth - in other words, knowledge exists outside divine revelation e.g. in physics, mathematics, medicine, psychology, etc., all of which are capable of being tested by the experience of this life.

Rational Christians are not opposed to such first principles of secularism, per se. Where Christians object is when radical secularist ideology is being adopted in current ways which threaten Christian rights, in government and political interventions, where humanistic philosophy and values infringe upon divinely held beliefs. Radical secularists go so far as to insist that all religion is to be regarded as a private matter for individuals for the home and place of worship, and that the state is to be blind to all religious doctrine.

Doctor Harvey Cox of Harvard Divinity School, the author of 'The Secular City' has written:

"We now live in a 'post-Christian' America. The Judeo-Christian ethic no longer guides our social institutions. Christian ideals and values no longer dominate social thought and action. The Bible has ceased to be a common base of moral authority for judging whether something is right or wrong, good or bad, acceptable or unacceptable."

To put it in very understandable words, Christians claim that radical secularism is now a religion unto itself, a religion in opposition to the freedoms of living out and demonstrating the mandate of the 'Way' - the teachings of Christ. In reality, secularism is a modern religion that professes to be non-religious, suppressing those who are religious!

Of course, radical secularists object to Christians claiming that they are religious members of a worldly organized religion. But a basic understanding of what it means to be a human being refutes such objections. I ask: "What does it mean to be religious"? Simply that one gives one's life over to some ideology, belief system, supreme goal - anything that takes dominion in one's life, that which comes first is one's value system.

Secular humanists deny that they are worshipping beings, but human beings are designed to worship. The fact is, everyone worships something, or someone, and organizes their life's practices around the matter of that affection.

Thus, everyone is religious! Even atheists are religious since they have given their lives over to a belief. The 'gods' to which secularists bow down are self-designed and manufactured, simply modern polytheism in our pluralistic society.

In short, in secular religion, the fundamentals of beliefs are innumerable since everyone is free to choose and engage faith in something - where faith can be defined as believing in whatever one chooses to believe, regardless of whether evidence exists to verify the actuality of such credence.

This then qualifies Christianity as a subset of contemporary culture. But this is precisely where the problems for Christians begin! As stated, Christians do not object to the most admirable and worthy aspects of secularism: raising money for the disadvantaged by holding public events to sponsor causes through sports, staging musical concerts and charging admission to sponsor worthy agendas, marches for worthy fundraising programs, organized philanthropic undertakings. Not at all!

Christians have always been taught to 'love one's neighbor as oneself.' Christians of all denominations willingly desire to be part of such benevolent causes! We do not wish to impose our values on those who disagree with us.

But where Christians object, strenuously protest, is that many of such secular events are purposely scheduled to take place on Sunday mornings - precisely during the set times of public worship in our churches, forcing worshippers to choose between the duty of worshipping God, versus participating in worthy secular causes.

So dear Christians, which must come first: the sacred or the secular? Only we ourselves can answer that question and we must answer it! This is why we Christians label secularism as anti-religious, even though secularism claims to advocate freedom of individual belief. We have been set-up to make choices that in the past we have never been required to make!

Back to my opening question: "What is a Christian to do?"

I leave you with two passages of Holy Scripture:

"All things are lawful, but not all things are beneficial." (1 Corinthians 10:23)

"Then give the emperor the things that are the emperor's and to God the things that are God's." (Luke 20:25)

Oh, by the way, will your children be in church and Sunday School this coming Sunday, or at soccer or baseball practice?

Christians, we must step out in the name of Christ! What do you think stepping out entails? Can we do it together? Yes, we can! For we Christians believe that the church should guide secular society, and not that secular society should dictate to the church. Since secularists say that they support the protection of individual believers, but not the protection of their beliefs, we must individually or collectively say 'yes' to what is of God in our modern age, and say 'no,' i.e. to step out, to not participate in what is contrary to Biblical teachings and church tradition! After all, St. Paul and the early Church Fathers who died in defense of the Church would expect nothing less of us!

All responses to this article can reach me by email to:

drangus@fastmail.com.

CHAPTER TWENTY-FIVE

ANGUS' article was the talk of the gathered thousand or so who met for the first ever multi-denominational Christian picnic in the town park. Curious about the coalition's term 'stepping out,' the Tangleville Mirror sent a reporter to the Saturday event.

The staff members of the twelve participating parishes had done a magnificent job in advertising and promoting the event. They had no idea how many might show up for the occasion, but were overwhelmed by the turnout of parents, children, grandparents and pew members of the various congregations. Everyone who attended was greeted by a member of the welcoming committee and given an agenda and a name tag on which to record his or her name and parish.

"You must meet and greet as many of the gathered crowd as possible," each attendee was told. "On the back of your name tag, record the names of the parishes you discover. The first person who gets the names of all twelve congregations recorded will win a prize. So don't just look around to greet those of your own congregation - mingle!"

And mingle they did, especially the children and teenagers. A twelve-year-old girl, Sarah, from St. Joseph's Roman Catholic parish, was the first to submit her form showing that she had met a parish member from all twelve participating congregations. Her prize was a pass to the movie of her choice at the downtown theatre and a ten-dollar coupon for the concession stand.

Sarah was delighted. In the process she met another girl, a member of St. Augustine's African Methodist Parish who also attended her dance class on Friday evenings; up until now neither knew the other was a church goer. They were about to become close friends.

In the morning session, a series of games were organized in which people of all ages were invited to sign up to participate: volleyball, foot races, relay races, croquet, horseshoe throwing, water balloon fights with balloons supplied by the local fire department, and the most popular of all, a search for a hidden treasure chest which contained a fifty-dollar gift certificate to a local restaurant.

The treasure chest was discovered by a ten-year-old boy named Moses, a member of Pastor Richard Head's Evangelical Community Church. He was the only child of a single parent mother, and he immediately informed the crowd that he would be taking his mom to dinner on her birthday next week. He received a lengthy round of applause from the gathered crowd.

The games ceased for the twelve o'clock smorgasbord luncheon set up on ten end-to-end picnic tables. Dr. Angus was asked to bless the food and after a short blessing a loud "Amen!" could be heard by passers-by on the sidewalk just outside the park entrance.

Each family attending the picnic had been instructed to bring enough food for themselves plus an additional four people. As a result, there was so much food that everyone was invited to second helpings. Families talked about being impressed by the variety of dishes, many which were indigenous to the cultures represented by the various church communities. There were little tags placed behind each dish to identify what the names of the individual dishes were. It was a learning experience all around. Father Ivan's Russian Orthodox parish food table was a favorite. Many folks had never tasted perogies. The recipe was requested by the mothers of children who asked why they weren't served in their own homes.

Dessert was ice cream topped off with chocolate syrup and whipped cream, all donated by the owner of Tangleville's Dairy Bar on Main Street, an affluent member of First Baptist Parish. Many of the young children needed to be washed up afterward - sticky hands and faces were everywhere!

An announcement had been sent out in advance of the day that a special offering would be taken up after lunch to augment the coffers of the 'Might of the Mite' fund. The children were advised to bring one coin, no larger than a twenty-five cent piece, to contribute to the fund. It seemed at the time to be a ho-hum request. It turned out to be the event of the day!

Then, at precisely one forty-five in the afternoon, a large flat-bed truck pulled into the park. On its bed was loaded a brightly coloured dunking tank. The fun was about to begin!

Harry Sting took the microphone of the portable public address system and began to inform the large crowd which had gathered around the surprise device what was about to take place.

"Ladies and Gentlemen, boys and girls: I hope that you didn't forget about the instructions that were sent to you that an offering would be accepted this afternoon to augment our 'Might of the Mite' benevolent fund. Well, that's exactly what we're going to do now. Only, we are going to make it a surprise way of collecting your donations. Here is how it's going to work!

"Each of the twelve clergy present today has agreed in advance to take a turn on the seat of the dunking tank … each for the ten minute, closely timed interval. For a twenty-five cent donation to the 'Might of the Mite' fund, you will have a chance to throw three balls at the target of the machine. Hit the target and the cleric will take a dunking. We will record the number of dunkings for each of the clerics … the winner will hold the title of 'the least dry preacher' in Tangleville. And we will start with giving the children here today the first throws. So line up boys and girls … form a queue and get ready to take aim.

"And by the way, the clergy have already drawn lots to determine the order of the sitting on the 'wet seat'. The first up is the Reverend Jim Adams from St. Timothy's Parish."

With Annie Sting holding the stop watch, the children scrambled to the starting line ready to take their aims at the twelve clerics. Each cleric was dressed in a bathing suit under an old choir gown from their home parish. There was a variety of colors waiting to get soaked.

The results were hilarious, with Harry recording the number of successful dunks for each cleric. The following results were recorded:

Cleric	Church	Dunks
Rev. Jim Adams	St. Timothy's Anglican	3
Fr. Thomas McCann	St. Joseph's Roman Catholic	2
Rev. James Johnson	St Augustine's African Methodist Episcopal	2
Rev. Mary Jones	First Pentecostal	3
Pastor Richard Head	Evangelical Community Church	5
Rev. Dieter Muller	St. Peter's Lutheran	3
Rev. Charles MacCormick	First Baptist	9

Major John Huff	Salvation Army Citadel	4
Fr. Ivan Fedosov	St. Vladimir's Orthodox	5
Canon Matthew Hudson	St. Bartholomew's Anglican	5
Fr. Leo Mahoney	St. Anne's Roman Catholic	6
Dr. Angus McLaughlin	St. Andrew's Presbyterian	7

It was obvious that the younger children had been successful in scrambling to the head of the line to begin the contest. Their aims were clearly inferior to the older youths who were then at the rear of the queue. After the last of the ten minute trials was concluded, it was announced that the Rev Charles McCormick of First Baptist Church was the winner with nine dunks.

When Harry handed him the microphone to accept his prize, Rev. Charles quipped, "The reason for my success is that we Baptists believe in full immersion for baptism. I guess it works here too, today!" The amused crowd gave him a sound round of applause.

Rev. Charles, after receiving his certificate for being 'the least dry preacher in Tangleville,' and ever the practical fundraiser, raised his hand to calm the applause, and exclaimed, "All of us clergy are now a little wet behind the ears, but there is one well-known celebrity here who is still as dry as when he arrived this morning: Harry Sting! Do you think that he should get off without being initiated in the dunk tank?"

A rousing "No!" arose from the crowd.

"All right now, I'm going to auction Harry off to the highest bidder here this afternoon. The highest bidder can take as many throws as necessary to dunk him. The proceeds, of course, will go to the 'Might of the Mite' fund. What do you say?"

The amused crowd began to chant, "Harry! Harry! Harry! Dunk Harry!"

Two of the off-duty members of the Tangleville Police Force, in civilian dress and members of the congregation of Canon Hudson's parish, closed in on Harry, escorted him to the seat of the dunk tank, placing him in view of the bemused crowd. Harry feigned objection to his mock arrest, but his clearly visible smile gave away that he was thoroughly enjoying every moment of the staged charade.

A surprise to the crowd, Rev. Charles, who'd been a professional auctioneer before his calling to ministry, began his chant, *"Hey, well, all right now, here we go there, and what are ya gonna give for him?"*

Annie, standing right in front of Rev. Charles, held up her hand and bid one hundred dollars. The crowd cheered and Rev. Charles continued, *"I'm bid one hundred dollar bidder, now two, now two, now two. Thank -you sir, now three."*

A man at the back of the crowd yelled, "Three hundred dollars!"

"I'm bid three hundred dollars bidder, would you give me four?"

Four hundred dollars, five hundred dollars, soon nine hundred dollars followed. Finally, the bidding was narrowed down to two contenders: the owner of the Tangleville Ford dealership and the owner of the John Deere dealership on the edge of the town. They knew each other, one being a member of St. Anne's Roman Catholic parish and the other a member of St. Joseph's Roman Catholic congregation. They were long-time golfing buddies, each always trying to upstage the other, but both refused to bid any higher.

Rev. Charles was having the time of his life. *"All right now, holding a nine hundred dollar bid. I'm bid nine hundred, two bidders. Would you give me one thousand?"*

Finally, one more hand went up, later to be identified as the owner of Tangleville Toyota.

"I've got one-thousand-dollar bidder! Now eleven, now eleven, now eleven. Who will make it eleven hundred? One thousand going once, one thousand going twice, fair warning! Sold to you, Madame, for one thousand dollars!"

The unidentified lady approached the throwing line accompanied by her husband, a tall lefty, wearing a baseball cap. He was, she announced, to be her relief pitcher for the occasion.

The man paused for a moment, reared back and fired the ball, directly hitting the trip mechanism of the dunking machine. Harry took his plunge to the bottom of the tank and the crowd broke into an extended applause. But who was that lefty?, everyone wondered.

CHAPTER TWENTY-SIX

THE next day, people at St. Bart's, who had been at the picnic had been good-naturedly asking Harry if he had dried off yet. And was he going to seek revenge against those Baptists, those full-immersion baptism supporters and their pastor?

"Just wait and see!" was all Harry would say, all the while sporting a smile that gave away that he was enjoying every minute of attention he was receiving.

Up early on Monday morning, the edition of The Tangleville Mirror arrived at 6:30 a.m. as usual, and with the newspaper and coffee, one cream, no sugar, in hand, Harry retired to his favorite chair on his back deck and settled down for one of his favorite daily rituals. His Monday radio show was scheduled for 10:00 a.m., and he wanted to be up on the latest news in Tangleville just in case someone should refer to a weekend happening in town.

It was the front page article that immediately caught his attention. A picture of Harry himself, at the bottom of the dunk tank, in full color, topped off Meddle's article.

WHAT IS TANGLEVILLE'S CHRISTIAN COMMUNITY UP TO?

By Maggie Meddle

Well over twelve hundred church goers attended a multi-denominational Stepping Out picnic at Tangleville's Community Park last Saturday. From all reports (I was there incognito), it was a rousing success.

There were games for all ages, a smorgasbord luncheon with such a variety of food, especially from the various ethnic churches, that labels were needed to inform people what was in the dishes. Contests, with prizes for the young folk and most popular of all, a dunking machine where twelve clergy were soaked, all for charity.

It seems that there is a new money raising scheme in town with a strange title – "The Might of the Mite." The gathered crowd seemed to understand the title, but for the life of me, it goes right over my head. Nevertheless, it was enthusiastically supported by the gathered Christians.

To my great surprise, the owner of Tangleville Toyota paid one thousand dollars to dunk AM KNOW's notorious Harry Sting. One has to ask, "What's going on with those Christians in town? Are we seeing the first of a concerted united uprising of religious popularism in Tangleville? What are their motives? Should we secularists be concerned?" If you have been following Dr. Angus McLaughlin's column entitled 'The Cleric Speaks', you'll note that perhaps we are being warned of the sleeping Christian community's intention to challenge the secular status quo.

The question is: "Is our liberal non-judgmental notion that all religions of the world are equal being challenged?" If so, heaven help us! All responses may be directed to me through my email: mmeddle @fastmail.com

"That's not a bad picture of me," Harry mused. "And that article, why it's the best piece of exposure that the coalition could possibly receive. And free too! I'm sure that the good people of Tangleville will want to comment on it during my show today.

In her housecoat and slippers, Annie arrived to take the chair next to his, coffee in hand. "What's that sly smile all about? You're up to something, aren't you?" she inquired.

"Here, read this," he said as he handed her the morning edition. "I've got to get to the radio station."

Prior to their arrival, Harry's guests for the morning had stopped for coffee together at the Bean Grinder. The Rev. Jim Adams from St. Timothy's Anglican Parish and Father Thomas McCann, rector of St. Joseph's Roman Catholic parish, were dressed in civilian clothes, not wanting to draw attention to themselves at the coffee shop as they used their time to plan their remarks on Harry's show. Both agreed that they would most likely be required to address Dr. McLaughlin's article in last Friday's Tangleville Mirror and the Maggie Meddle column in today's edition. They were in agreement that today's show must thoroughly clarify the concept of stepping out. Harry was waiting in his office for their arrival and warmly received them.

Harry quizzed his guests on what they expected to be confronted with on the show, and when they explained their plan of clarifying the concept of stepping out he readily agreed. Together, they walked into the broadcast booth and settled down for the show to begin. Harry was smiling from ear to ear. This was going to be a broadcast for Tangleville's audience to remember well into the future!

The On Air light flashed on and Harry began: "Good morning thinking people of Tangleville. Welcome to today's show! My special guests before me are two well-known clerics of the town, The Rev. Fr. Thomas McCann, Rector of St. Joseph's Roman Catholic Parish, and The Rev. Fr. Jim Adams, the priest at St. Timothy's Anglican Parish.

Gentlemen, thank you for coming today. Have we got a lot to talk about this morning! So, are you ready to table some answers to the flood of emails I've received over the weekend?"

Fr. Jim and Fr. Thomas, in unison, answered, "we are," each giving the thumbs up sign to Harry across the desk. Harry winked back at them.

"Let's start with Dr. McLaughlin's article in last Friday's edition of the Tangleville Mirror. Dr. Angus claims that Christians are getting a raw deal in today's secular society, that they are in fact undergoing a form of modern persecution. Do you agree?"

"He's right on, Harry! It certainly is not politically correct for me to say so, but it's so blatant that we Christians of all denominations are frustrated with how times have changed over the past three to four decades," responded Fr. Jim.

"How so?"

Fr. Thomas signalled that he was eager to get into the conversation, adding, "Christians are presently having to make choices that they, in the past, have never been forced to do."

"You had better explain, Fr. Thomas."

"Let me begin with what society used to call the Lord's Day. Sunday mornings in the weekly calendar were times when Christian families went to church. It was a day of family get-togethers, rest and relaxation, a time for paying 'spiritual taxes,' so to speak, by being in the pews. Not all in society, by any means were church goers, but Sundays were still special to society at large. Even the non-practising who did not adhere to Christian Sabbath norms reserved a time-out for the faithful to worship. Not so now!

"Contemporary society now considers Sunday mornings as times of the week to hold a multitude of secular events, fund raisers of every kind, sporting events, practice times for our youth to prepare for future games: hockey, baseball, soccer. Add to these events fundraising walk-a-thons, bicycle family outings, art displays in the park, so called boating poker runs to raise money for various worthwhile charities. The list goes on and on!"

"But Fr. Thomas, are not all of these activities notable and worthwhile activities? Surely you would agree that such events are a benefit to society?"

"Of course we agree, Harry. In fact, most Christians would take part as well in such laudable endeavors, but to do so forces us to make a choice between our allegiances to God at public worship versus our desire to assist in good causes. We can't do both at the same time."

"Let me push this a little farther, Fathers. What do you mean by an 'allegiance to God?'"

"Harry," Father Jim was quick to pick up the conversation, "We clergy have published a document called The Tangleville Christian Coalition Manifesto, a document that has been endorsed by all twelve of Tangleville's Christian denominations. It consists of ten statements which we Christians maintain are self-evident. Number two reads as follows:

'That it is the will of God that every baptised Christian live out the mandate of Christ stated in St. Mark's Gospel: '*The first is this, 'Hear, O Israel: the Lord our God, the Lord is one; you shall love the Lord your God with all your heart, and with all your soul, and with all your mind, and with all your strength. The second is this, You shall love your neighbour as Yourself.*' (Mark 12:29-31)

"In simple language, Harry, that means we Christians 'pray before we play.' God comes first, always, before the other demands of life push in on us. We can do no other!"

"And that, Harry," chimed in Fr. Thomas, "means we must miss out on participating in perfectly worthy secular causes, because we are in church where such attitudes begin."

Fr. Jim continued, "You see, Christianity and secular cultures do not by nature walk at times on the same paths, nor hold similar values. We must 'render to Caesar the things that are Caesar's and to God the things that are of God.'"

Harry grinned at his two guests as he deliberately waited out a few seconds of dead air, and then asked, "So how are you people going to address this?"

This was the question the two clerics were waiting for in the show. They had rehearsed how they were going to answer such a question: "By stepping out, Harry. By stepping out," they answered in unison.

There were another few seconds of dead air. Father Jim broke the silence, saying, "We Christians are not naïve. We know that we cannot impose our values on society. We have no power, no right, nor mandate to compel others to follow Christ. We simply can only influence others by example. So we have decided to exercise our rights and freedoms in an open democratic society by refusing to participate in what we feel is contrary to proper Christian decrees. We call it Stepping Out. Who can possibly criticize such a non-violent solution?

On December 5, 1955, The Rev. Dr. Martin Luther King, in a major speech to the American people said, 'There comes a time when people get tired.' He of course was referring to racial injustice. A modified version of that statement applies to contemporary Christians.

There comes a time when we Christians get tired of being ignored by secular society. For too long, Harry, compliance was much easier than resistance. We have put up with being brushed off to our own detriment. Now we are going to again become visible in our town. Together we are far more numerous than people believe. We're going to step out together," summed up Fr. Thomas.

"Flesh this out for me and my listeners," Harry asked.

"We're not aiming to be a diversion in Tangleville. We will always be non-violent peacemakers, subject to the laws and authorities of society," responded Fr. Thomas. "But what we will strive to do is become a second wave to secular functions which we feel have become worthy of our participation. For instance, if a marathon walk for charity is scheduled for 10:00 a.m. on a Sunday morning, and we Christians wish to participate, we will 'pray before we play'. We will first go to worship during our regular times of gathering and then meet at an appointed time after lunch to do our 'Christian wave' for the event. Who says that starting times are so set that participants cannot start at a later hour? We will pray before we play! And I can't imagine that the monies raised by our second wave of participation will be unwelcome!"

"So," Harry asked, "stepping out does not necessarily mean opposing society's events?"

"No, not at all," replied Fr. Jim. "It means that we Christians will participate or choose not to do so, in secular occurrences, on our own terms. We will simply be making joint statements that we're not invisible communities to be ignored. The church does not need more preachers. What it needs are more practitioners.

Stepping out is our way of saying we will do it our way if we choose to participate in secular society's worthy causes. And vice versa, if we decide to not participate in such activities which contemporary culture applauds, we simply remain 'out of step' with the status quo. We still live in a free country! Living the Christian life is not a private matter!"

"Harry," added Fr. Thomas, "there is also a corollary to the term 'stepping out.' It can also mean initiating our own events, activities, and occasions for a Christian presence in society: parades, social functions, sporting events, picnics, our own fundraising projects. Special seasons of the church calendar - Christmas, Easter, and Pentecost - need to be times of celebrations for Christians demonstrated in ways beyond what is practised inside our church buildings. These festivals need to become visible to society at large. We will be working on how to reintroduce Christian high days to a public largely untutored in such sacred celebrations."

The control room engineer was frantically signalling to Harry that a commercial break was coming up. Harry waved to him and cut off the conversation. "Ladies and gentlemen, we will now break for a commercial. Don't go away! We'll be right back!"

"Great stuff guys!" he told them as the broadcast went to commercial. "We've got only eight minutes left for this half hour of the show. Where do you want to go from here?"

"Why don't you ask us about Maggie Meddle's article?" suggested Fr. Thomas.

An office employee rushed in with three cups of steaming coffee, cream and sugar on the side. The On Air light flashed on as the three were sipping their hot drinks. "We're back folks," said Harry. "Thank you for waiting. I've got one more question today for our guests. What did you make of Maggie Meddle's article in today's newspaper?"

Fr. Jim was first to respond. "Harry, wasn't it a typical indictment on our secular age when she didn't know the meaning of the word 'mite'? Any Sunday School child would be able to answer that. It of course, refers to Jesus' observation of the poor widow dropping all she had, two mites, two copper coins, into the temple treasury. See how far contemporary society has drifted from a Biblical awareness?

"And, Harry, the best argument for our stance on stepping out on your show today was her statement that she was worried that the sleeping churches were intent on challenging the secular status quo - and then ending her article by stating 'heaven help us.' What a paradox! She doesn't want religion to be a challenge to the conscience of contemporary society, and then ends by invoking the presence of heaven!"

"Gentlemen," Harry said, "it has been a delight to have you as our guests this morning. I have the feeling that the term 'stepping out' will become a household phrase in Tangleville, both by a united church community and by the disciples of Maggie Meddle. Thank you for coming, and God bless you!"

The ON AIR sign flashed off.

"Wasn't that a dead giveaway Harry of where you stand, your statement, 'God bless you?'" asked Fr. Jim.

"I'm simply stepping out, Fathers. "Simply stepping out!"

CHAPTER TWENTY-SEVEN

IT had been two weeks since Harry had been unceremoniously dunked in that water tank. He was still savoring the event. Each of the clergy who had gone through the procedure had been forewarned of the event. They each knew that they were going to sit on the wet seat of the device, but no one had leaked information to Harry that he was going to be required to do likewise. They had each gone prepared with a bathing suit and an old parish choir gown to cover themselves.

But not Harry! He was only given the opportunity to hand over his billfold and wristwatch to Annie before taking his turn. He had no time to change his clothes or to remove his shoes before his dunking. He took it all in great fun. What pleased him the most was that the owner of Tangleville Toyota, he was told, paid one thousand dollars for the privilege of being his official dunker. One thousand dollars to add to the 'Might of the Mite' benevolent fund!

But Harry, being Harry, who liked to always be in control and in the know, didn't personally know the owner of the Toyota dealership and was curious. To which parish did she belong? And who was that lefty who'd thrown that single dead-center pitch to dunk him? He couldn't take it any longer. He had to find out more information about them. Curiosity was one of his traits, for better or for worse.

Harry picked up the phone in his office at AM KNOW and dialed the number of Tangleville Toyota. The automatic answering picked up, "Good morning! Tangleville Toyota! If you wish to speak with a salesperson, dial 1. For a maintenance appointment, dial 2. For parts, dial 3. For collision repairs, dial 4. To speak to the operator, dial 0."

Harry dialed 0 and waited.

"Good morning, Janice speaking. How may I help you?"

Harry, using his professional radio voice, and an air of authority, responded,

"I wish to speak to the owner of the dealership."

"Whom shall I say is calling?"

"Mr. Harry Sting from AM KNOW"

There was a long pause. Harry was certain that the operator was conversing with the owner before passing him through.

"Hello Mr. Sting. Amelia Pennington speaking."

Harry immediately jotted down her name on his note pad before him. Should he address her by her first name or by her surname? He chose to go the informal route.

"Amelia, this is Harry Sting from AM KNOW. Thankyou for taking my call. Let me be up front and tell you that this is not an official interview call, nor is it being recorded. I am simply calling to personally say thank you for the one thousand dollar donation which you made to the 'Might of the Mite' Fund two weeks ago at the multi-denominational Church picnic at Tangleville Park. We really appreciate your generosity!"

"Why thanks, Mr. Sting! It was my privilege to do so!"

Harry could sense a change of tone in Amelia's voice. It was almost as if she was responding with some relief in her reply. Harry knew from experience that when people suspect that they are being taped by the media for an interview that they demonstrate stress, even fear, in their speaking demeanor.

"Amelia, please call me Harry. I trust that it is okay if I call you by your first name – especially since I've already done so."

"That's just fine, Harry. Now, how can I help you?"

Harry, after years of interviewing people on his radio show, immediately detected that Amelia was not one for small talk and wasting time. Clearly she was in control of the call!

"Amelia, I must confess that I'm an active participant in the newly established Tangleville Christian Clergy Coalition here in town. We gather information about those who participate in our Stepping Out objective, as outlined in our published manifesto. Do you mind if I ask you a few questions?"

"You may ask, Harry, and I'll answer those which I feel are fair and appropriate. How's that?"

Harry agreed, and could sense that he had better ask a softball question to begin his unofficial interview. "Why you were willing to pay one thousand dollars to dunk me in that tank?" Harry waited for her to respond, not quite sure how she would answer the question.

"Because, Harry, I wanted to cool you off in some cold water!"

There was a long silence. How should he take that answer? Was it a joke? A criticism of some sort?

He decided to play her game, "Amelia, if I had not been able to surface that day, would you have been willing to step in, get wet yourself, and pull me to safety?"

Amelia laughed - she clearly got Harry's quick wit.

"Of course Harry! I want you to know that I agree with 99% of what you say on the radio. I'm simply implying that there are many out there who think that your opinions are all wet. I'm not one of them, though."

"Amelia, point well taken. But I think that you must be on board with us to make such a donation. To which denomination here in Tangleville are you an adherent?"

"I'm a member of the Rev. James Johnson's St. Augustine congregation, the African Methodist Episcopal denomination, ever since I married my husband Lefty. He's of African descent and I'm white. We are so freely welcomed there. That's not the case within all Christian denominations!"

"Amelia, I can assure you that that's something we in the Coalition are doing our best to rectify. There is no place for racism in Christianity. Tell me a little more about Lefty. That was quite a curve ball he threw that got you your wish!"

"His name is Lawrence Jones, but everyone simply called him Lefty when he played professional ball in the United States. He retired a couple of years ago and now works for me here at the dealership in Tangleville."

"I'd sure like to meet him, Amelia. Do you suppose that would be possible?"

"He's right here in my office. I'll turn the phone over to him. Thank you for calling."

"Lefty speaking!"

"Lefty, this is Harry Sting over at AM KNOW. This is not an official interview - I'm sure that as a professional baseball player you've had your share of them. But I want you to know that I was really impressed with that throw of yours that dunked me two weeks ago. A curve ball, right?"

"No, it was a fast ball. It did the trick, didn't it?"

"I was impressed! And so were the twelve clergy who were at the picnic. We would like to meet you in person." Harry was flying by the seat of his pants in the conversation at this point.

"Do you think that you could spare an hour or so of your time and meet with us next Wednesday at 10:00 a.m.? We'll be meeting at your parish downtown. We have a proposition to make to you."

"Harry, I'm retired now and enjoying every day of it. But yes, I can be there. Can you tell me what the meeting is all about?"

"I'd rather wait for the rest of the group to be present. Is that okay?"

Harry wanted to plant a little mystery in the mind of Mr. Jones. Besides, he wasn't quite sure where he was going with this invitation for Lefty to be present at the upcoming meeting. But by next Wednesday, he was certain that he would be able to come up with a proposal to present to the twelve clerics. Lefty's skills were just too good to not be put into some constructive use for Tangleville's developing Stepping Out agenda.

CHAPTER TWENTY-EIGHT

HARRY was having second thoughts about his invitation to Lefty Jones to meet with the clerics at St. Augustine. It wasn't that he had reservations about Lefty coming - not at all. What was of concern was that he hadn't cleared it with the clergy first. Perhaps the agenda for the meeting had already been set. Would the group of twelve be troubled by this impulsive intervention for the morning?

In the back of his mind was percolating a role for Lefty to play in the development of a sporting component for Tangleville's youth. He wasn't yet clear as to how such an undertaking was to materialize, yet Harry was convinced that once the group was introduced to such an idea, and were to meet Lefty, that it would all come into focus.

There was one way to cover his misstep: an email to each of the twelve clerics seeking their permission to meet Lefty. Harry sat before his computer and composed his request:

To: Tangleville's Twelve Apostles
Re: Proposal and request
Greetings,

Yesterday I called Amelia Pennington, the owner of Tangleville Toyota, and thanked her for the one thousand dollar donation to the 'Mite of the Mite' Fund. I learned that she and her husband, Lefty, are members of St. Augustine parish, the very place where we are scheduled to meet this coming Wednesday. But here is what really excited me: her husband, Lefty, is a retired professional baseball player, a pitcher, the fellow who threw that fast ball that saturated me in that dunking tank at our picnic. I'm convinced that he could have a leadership role to play in some sporting events for youth here in our own town if we invite him to do so. Do I have your permission to invite him to join with us this coming Wednesday? I believe that we have the perfect guy to initiate an outreach component in our Stepping Out plans.

Please answer ASAP!

Harry

Harry's anxiety meter dropped a few levels as he pressed 'send'. If the clerics object, he would still have time to call Lefty and perhaps arrange for another meeting approved by the clerical membership. If they outright objected to him coming, Harry would invite Lefty to lunch instead of being himself present at the meeting.

* * *

The sound of Canon Hudson's cell phone necessitated a quick pulling into the parking lot of a downtown fast food restaurant.

"Canon Hudson speaking."

"Canon, this is Audrey Holmes. I'm calling from the hospital downtown. Jack has just been admitted to emergency with a brain hemorrhage. The doctor tells me that he isn't going to survive. Can you come right away to be with us?"

"I'm downtown right now. I'll be there in about ten minutes. Can he speak at the present time?"

"No, he is completely unconscious. I don't know what to do. Please hurry."

"Stay with him. I'm on my way."

Canon Hudson was only three blocks from the Tangleville hospital. He pulled into the parking lot, grabbed his prayer book and communion kit and dashed into the emergency section of the building. Being a well-known cleric in the institution, he was greeted by the receptionist on duty who was expecting his arrival. Audrey had called down that her priest was on his way.

"Canon, I'm told we only have a few minutes before Jack will pass on. I know that he has made his peace with the Lord. I'm not worried about his eternal future. But I'm scared. We've been together for over forty-five years. I don't want to let him go even though I accept that he is in God's hands. I'm so glad that you are here!"

They held each other for a few seconds saying nothing, Canon Hudson simply comforting Audrey. He broke the silence and said, "Audrey, I brought the oil for last rites. Do you want me to anoint Jack for dying?"

"Oh, please Canon. By all means. I'm so glad that you got here before his passing."

Audrey and Canon Matthew, on opposite sides of Jack's bed, joined together in the holding of Jack's hands for a time of silent prayer. It was a procedure that Canon Hudson had done countless times in the past at the bedside of a dying Christian.

Canon Hudson broke the silence with the following prayer from the prayer book: *"God of mercy, look with love on Jack and receive him into your heavenly kingdom. Bless him and let him live with you forever. We ask this grace through Christ the Lord. Amen."*

Audrey remained standing, tears in her eyes, as Canon Matthew read the 23rd Psalm and offered a prayer for the dying Jack and for the comfort and peace of Audrey.

He concluded the service with the following traditional words from the Anglican liturgy, anointing Jack with the holy oil of unction, blessed by the Bishop at the last Maundy Thursday Eucharist:

> "God of mercy, into whose hands your Son Jesus Christ
> commended His spirit at his last hour, into those same
> hands we now commend your servant Jack that death
> may be for him the gate to life and eternal fellowship
> with you; through Jesus Christ our Lord. Amen."

Canon Hudson and Audrey remained in silence on either side of Jack. It was a time of waiting until Jack passed on to meet his Lord. In the interval, a nurse popped in to check on Jack, and generously volunteered to bring the two a coffee. They readily accepted.

Within the next twenty minutes, Jack breathed his final breath. It seemed like an easy passage.

The doctor asked the two of them to temporarily leave while he attended to his duties which occur at the time of death. Audrey and Canon Hudson were then invited to return to Jack's bedside.

When Audrey was ready to talk, they briefly discussed her plans for the days ahead: visitation at the funeral home, the possible date for the funeral. Canon Hudson knew that it was not the time for specific details - they could come later. Now it was important for Audrey to make her departure from the hospital. She was going to spend the next few hours with her daughter and son-in-law on the west end of town.

Canon Hudson walked her to her car, and promised to meet with her and the family as soon as they were ready to make decisions for the coming days ahead.

Canon Matthew was exhausted. He had conducted many such services of last rites at the bedsides of the dying. It was such a privilege to do so. But it always took its toll on his emotional well-being. As he drove back to the office of St. Bart's he, in a silent prayer, asked God for strength and guidance in the coming days for Audrey and the family.

CHAPTER TWENTY-NINE

AUDREY Holmes and the family decided on two nights of visitation at the downtown Tangleville Funeral Chapel, Monday and Tuesday gatherings for friends and acquaintances to pay their respects to Jack's passing. Audrey was overwhelmed by the number of people who came, especially parishioners from St. Bartholomew's parish. It's at such times that the church always stands in solidarity with those who grieve.

The funeral celebration of Jack's life was scheduled for 10:00 a.m. on Wednesday morning with Canon Hudson officiating. Audrey had first considered holding the funeral in St. Bart's Church, but because Jack, during his lifetime was not a regular church attendee, she felt it would be more appropriate to gather at the funeral home instead of a parish setting where the Eucharist would normally be celebrated.

Following the short graveside service of committal, everyone was invited for a time of fellowship back in the parish hall at St. Bart's. The ladies of the women's guild provided the luncheon with Canon Hudson and Maggie in attendance. Father Matthew said the blessing before the gathered crowd sat down to eat.

Audrey, it was obvious to all, was exhausted as she thanked everyone for the support which she and the family had received during the days following Jack's passing. She positively felt the love extended by the parish family and friends during a very stressful time in her life. In the days following the funeral, the many cards and letters in the mail brought tears to her eyes. Jack was no longer her earthly partner, but she found solace in the knowledge of his bedside baptism following his time of confession and absolution with Canon Hudson. She, in Christian faith, knew that someday, in God's good time, they would be reunited!

* * *

Canon Hudson arrived late at St. Augustine African Methodist Parish to join the already gathered clergy for the Wednesday scheduled meeting of the clerical coalition. The luncheon was just over when Matthew arrived, but dessert and coffee were waiting for him. Rev. James Johnson, the parish minister had received Matthew's email informing him that he would arrive as soon as he could get away following the morning funeral and reception, and James, a close friend of Matthew, in his reply, promised he would have a slice of chocolate cake waiting at his arrival.

The agenda for the meeting was circulated and at the top of the list of items was 'Harry Sting and Guest.' Harry took the floor and thanked the group for getting back so promptly by email giving him permission to bring along Lefty Jones. Lefty was seated at Harry's right at the table. The only cleric Jones knew personally was his own minister, the Rev. James Johnson, the host of today's gathering.

Harry was in his element as he invited Lefty to stand and, one by one, introduced by name each of the other eleven clerics. Lefty smiled and repeated the first name of each cleric as they were introduced to him. He was then invited to be seated as Harry outlined who his guest was and why he wanted him to be present.

"We have a celebrity in our presence today, my friends. Lefty Jones was the fellow who threw that fast ball and dunked me in that tank last week. Now you need to know why it took him only one throw to do it! He is a retired professional baseball pitcher, having played for a major farm team in the U.S. He just happens to be the spouse of Amelia Pennington, the owner of Tangleville Toyota, who paid a thousand dollars to have him throw that fateful pitch that soaked me to the skin."

The entire group of clerics burst into spontaneous applause with hoots of approval. Harry then proceeded to thank Lefty for coming today, and then cautiously, but skilfully, began to reveal his reasons why he was so anxious to have his guest present at the luncheon.

He began by saying, "After I watched Lefty throw the fast ball and then learned of his professional career in baseball, I had a brain wave that just kept getting more and more intriguing by the day. I ask, what are we Christians doing for our youth and our young athletes in Tangleville? We object to our kids being asked to attend sports practices during Sunday worship hours, asking them to 'pray before they play,' but in so doing we are sidelining some of them from playing on teams in town. I don't think we can continue to justifiably ask our youth to make such choices: a choice between their Christian faith and perhaps a future in a professional athletic career. I propose that we can remedy the situation."

"We're listening," responded Dr. McLaughlin.

"What if we were to set up our own leagues in town? Baseball, then perhaps hockey, soccer, lacrosse - girl's and boy's teams, both for youth and adults? Imagine a number of baseball teams for our youth where the players on each team consist of members from our twelve denominational congregations, all playing on mixed denominational teams. We could do the same for a number of adult teams. We would schedule practices and game times on Sunday afternoons and evenings throughout the week - maybe even eventually play against teams from another town. Can you imagine a better way for individuals from our twelve denominations to get to know one another, then playing together, intermingling and breaking down preconceived ideas about our faiths?"

"Let's get this straight, Harry," inquired Fr. Fedosov. "Are you foreseeing leagues to eventually challenge existing secular teams in the town? Do you want to pit our Christian players against Tangleville's official clubs?"

"It could happen," responded Harry, his impish smile showing through.

"What about prospective players who don't attend any of our twelve congregations but who wish to join a team?" asked Pastor Head.

"Ah, that is exactly what we should hope to take place. There should be an opportunity for practising Christians as well as possible new converts to play together. The secular world doesn't know much about people of 'The Way.' What better way to spread the good news of the Kingdom than to have people volunteer to be in our company?"

"What happens if Tangleville's existing baseball teams want to recruit some of the best players from our leagues? What do we do then?" inquired Canon Hudson.

"Wouldn't that be the perfect opportunity for such talented players to say, 'Yes, but only if I can attend worship at my church before going to your practice. 'First I pray, then I play.'" What a witness that would be to secular culture - the perfect opportunity for a Christian to step out for his or her convictions," Harry answered.

Question after question was directed at Harry. It was obvious that the clerics were interested in the idea, but unsure of how the adventure could be initiated.

Harry waited for the question that he needed to be asked: "Who can we obtain to oversee such an undertaking, that is, if we should approve to go full steam into such an ambitious project? Harry was ready. He deliberately affected a pause to intensify the importance of an answer, then turned to his guest, Lefty, at his side.

"Lefty, could you see yourself taking on the responsibility of being the ringleader in this ambitious but badly needed project? Who in Tangleville has more talent and experience than yourself?"

It was obvious that Lefty was taken totally by surprise by Harry's question. Before he could answer, the entire group of clerics began to applaud. They stood to their feet and gathered around the one person who clearly was the most qualified and perfect fit for the undertaking.

"Lefty, we would be honoured if you could see yourself to accept," said Dr. Angus.

There was a pregnant pause from Lefty. Finally, he spoke: "I'm honoured! Yes! I'll do my best. But, we will need start up money for gloves, bats, balls, you know, sweaters, equipment. Can we acquire such things?"

"Lefty," beamed Harry, taking his hand in his own, "we can and we will! You lead us in the oversight duties and we will do our financial part. This is an answer to our collective prayers. To all our prayers!"

Stepping Out had taken a gigantic step - the first major step among the many more Harry was sure were to come. On the way home from the meeting, his mind was set on dreaming up the name for the men's senior ball team. Why not the Tangleville Templars? But he knew that he had better wait to let Lefty work his magic first.

CHAPTER THIRTY

SIXTEEN months had passed since that meeting at St. Augustine African Methodist Episcopal Church. The twelve clergy and Harry Sting continued to meet semi-monthly for lunch. With the various parishes taking turns to host the gatherings, Stepping Out was now an expression and concept that was so well established and recognized in Tangleville, that both the secular and religious communities by now accepted its objective as established reality in town, and far beyond the Tangleville populace.

Lefty Jones' oversight and managerial skills in establishing baseball teams and tournaments for the youth and two adult teams were leveraged to an outstanding success. The four multi-denominational youth teams, each with volunteer coaches from the Christian communities, played each other weekly. The competition was fierce!

The two adult teams, The Tangleville Templars and the Tangleville Saints played against each other once a week; for the last four months, each team also played out of town against other Christian teams from two nearby communities.

Lefty's apprehensions about acquiring enough money to buy equipment were quickly obliterated through the generous donations from owners of businesses in town: Tangleville Ford, Tangleville Toyota, the local John Deere dealership, a donation from the Might of the Mite benevolent fund, along with many private contributions from individuals in the pews. The Tangleville Mirror was now regularly posting the scores of the teams in the sports section of the newspaper. The Christian community was now a recognized and active entity in Tangleville not fully applauded by everyone, yet nevertheless a presence that was projected in a fashion that before was all but silent.

Six months ago, hockey teams were established in the same make-up, multi-denominational in composition. All games were played during times that did not coincide with public worship. Sporting activities had brought the various denominations together, in a fashion that before was never thought possible. The Christians were now being talked about as a unified entity, not as divided denominational subsections of New Testament interpretation.

Interdenominational co-operation did not end with the development of sporting activities. With the realization that the Christian presence in Tangleville was being felt in ways that previously had not been acknowledged, the clergy and laity were soon to capitalize on their new-found dynamism.

They applied for a permit to enter a float in the annual Santa Claus parade and permission was granted. Volunteers from the parishes together designed and built the float which was drawn by a tractor supplied by the John Deere dealership. Youth representatives from all the churches were overjoyed to ride on the four-kilometre downtown and suburban route. The entry took first prize for both design and presentation.

Encouraged by this accomplishment, the churches decided to stage a collaborative live Christmas crèche setting consisting of real animals, actors, and a crude barn and manger setting with a real live young child representing the baby Jesus. The display was set up in one of the downtown local parks, open to the public from 6 to 11 p.m. two weeks before December 25th.

Volunteers staffed the display for two-hour periods while dressed in period costumes of Jesus' day. More church members volunteered than could actually be used. Mothers in particular were all too willing to have their infant children play the role of baby Jesus. It was the talk of the town.

The local television station ran a review of the presentation during a 6 p.m. news broadcast. The Tangleville Mirror wrote a glowing report of the event. Of course, Dr. McLaughlin featured the achievement in his Friday column, 'The Cleric Speaks.' The Christian community was getting noticed in a fashion that was both positive and affirmed. But not by all in the town!

Letters to the editor of the Tangleville Mirror were mixed in tone. The secularists were outraged over the amount of coverage that the Christians were receiving by the media. What was interesting was that the formerly divided denominations were never before considered as a threat to the worldly morals and activities of modern society. As long as the individual denominations continued to function as isolated pockets of Christendom, their divided numbers were never noticeable as alternative voices. But with the formation of the Tangleville Christian Coalition, their combined presence was becoming a force to contend with. This had never happened before in Tangleville.

Instead of the Methodists, or the Romans, or the Lutherans, indeed any of the various denominations independent of one another making news, now the media reported on 'the Christians,' not the separate denominations as newsmakers. Now their public presence in Tangleville involved large numbers of adherents. It was a vocal and visible group which possibly could challenge the status quo. It was becoming apparent for some that their slogan Stepping Out must be considered as a foreboding indication of change in town.

A letter to the editor was printed to that effect in the Mirror one Tuesday:

Christians: What Are They Up To?

"Something is happening in my town that I perceive is an intentional attempt to stifle the freedom of individual conscience and choice of lifestyle in Tangleville. The long cherished principle of separation of church and state is, I am afraid, being eroded, slowly but steadily by the Christian Coalition. Their united activities are now so effective, that what was once considered as our normal Sunday with public shopping and social events are now being seriously challenged. They refuse to participate in any activity that takes place during Sunday worship hours … they have set up their own sports events in town … they have arranged for religious public displays on their theological calendars (e.g. Christmas and Easter themes). It seems that all of it is being promoted by the local media.

Enough is enough! What are they up to. Are they trying to reverse the clock of our modern secular progressive age? Karl Marx wrote in 1843 that 'religion is the opium of the people.' I am afraid that Christianity is once again attempting to redesign our way of life which we now call tolerant and accepting. If only there was a god…I would say god help us!"

Molly Nitterworth,

President of The Freedom From Religion Organization

Dr. Angus read the letter with interest. Nitterworth had inadvertently supplied the theme for his next column, a topic which he judged was too good to be postponed.

CHAPTER THIRTY-ONE

WITH Molly Nitterworth's letter to the editor of the Tangleville Mirror before him, Dr. McLaughlin sat down before his computer to compose his weekly column. He was well aware that Molly's article was divisive amongst the town's populace. He and many of the other Christians who read it were slightly amused by her interpretation of what the Tangleville Christian Coalition's expression of stepping out actually involved. It was time to clarify the matter.

THE CLERIC SPEAKS

by The Rev. Dr. Angus McLaughlin

Dear People of Tangleville:

It is one thing to fully understand a movement and to rationally disagree with it. It is quite another to misjudge and to unjustly criticize. Such is the latter case, I'm afraid, when it comes to evaluating Ms. Molly Nitterworth's recent letter to the editor of this newspaper entitled 'Christians, What Are They Up To?'

Methinks that she has mistaken the slogan 'Stepping Out' for 'Stepping On.' There is a world of difference between the two expressions!

Three years ago the Christian Churches of Tangleville adopted what is now a document familiar to the majority of our community. It was entitled 'The Tangleville Christian Coalition Manifesto', and began with the preamble, 'We, the Christian clergy and laity of Tangleville, hold the following statements to be self-evident.' It is not my intent to republish these ten paragraphs in this column. However, it seems necessary to clarify the gist of the document.

Nowhere in the ten paragraphs does the document indicate, advise, or aim to "stifle the freedom of individual conscience and choice of lifestyle," as Ms. Nitterworth puts it. Nowhere does the document advise Christians to attempt to coerce non-believers to become converts to the faith. Nowhere is violence, intimidation, or intolerance in any fashion or form suggested against secular society. Quite the opposite in fact!

Christians are advised to be non-judgmental of others, pledging to work together to live out the teachings of Christ: to "give (render) unto the emperor Caesar the things that are the emperor's and to God the things that are God's." In other words, to 'step out' from participating in what is perceived as secular society's agenda, while living peacefully within the general population fully adhering to the laws of the land, but opting out from matters which violate their perceived Christian principles.

The objective of the Manifesto is Christian unity of outward expression by the various church denominations. It in no way attempts to suggest a single worship style when it comes to liturgical practises.

Again, freedom of choice for individual conduct within the limits of the laws of the country, freedom to worship God or not to do so, freedom of individual conscience in matters of personal belief with the freedom to express such choices, providing the law permits... these are the same values Christians hold and wish to practice. To opt out of any of the aforementioned is the right of individuals in a free and democratic nation, providing groups and individuals are willing to pay the consequences of doing so.

So Christians simply are demanding the same equal rights as all other members of secular society. They simply ask, "Why is secular society condemning us for doing so?" 'Stepping out' simply means to be visible, to be vocal exercising the right to be different from the status quo, to say 'yes' or to say 'no' to commonly accepted behaviour and conduct considered normal at the present time in history. Christians argue that without established divine authority in matters of morals, values, and personal conduct, anything and everything is eventually possible, provided the majority of the population decrees such matters as acceptable and legal. Be assured, Ms. Nitterworth, we Christians would never deny you the right to live out your life as you choose to do so. We simply ask that we be permitted to right to do likewise. Stepping 'out' does not include stepping 'on' you or anyone else. We, however, believe that God, through Jesus Christ has mandated the superior way to live – individually, collectively, and with one's neighbour.

In opposition to the concluding sentence in your article, I close by saying: "Believing that there 'is'a God, we say, God bless you!"

All responses to this article can reach me by email to:

drangus@fastmail.com.

Dr. Angus leaned back in his huge leather office chair and stretched. His second cup of coffee was now cold. It was almost time for lunch. The ringing of the telephone on his desk jarred him back to the realization that he had better attend to his church administration duties.

"Dr. Angus speaking!"

"Good morning Angus. This is Harry Sting. What are you doing for lunch today?"

"I haven't had time to think about it. Why? What's on your mind?"

"Let me pick you up in about fifteen minutes. I need to talk with you," replied Harry.

"You're on, Harry. But first we will have to stop off at the bank. I'm financially embarrassed, so to speak!"

"Don't worry! Lunch is on me! By the way, Father Leo and Canon Matthew are coming with us."

Dr. Angus re-read his article for the second time, found two spelling mistakes, and after correcting two grammatical errors, sent it in. Lunch with Harry and the two clerics would be a welcomed outing.

Chapter Thirty-Two

HARRY picked up Dr. Angus at St. Andrew's and together they drove to the Cantonese House of Gourmet, an upscale Chinese restaurant in downtown Tangleville. They entered and Harry was greeted by Wang, the Maître d'.

"Good morning, Mr. Sting. Your table of four is waiting."

It was obvious to Dr. Angus that Harry must be a regular at the restaurant to be so readily recognized and that he had made a reservation for the luncheon.

"Wang, I have two other guests coming today, two clerics. Please show them to our table when they arrive."

"Certainly, Mr. Sting. It is always great to see you. How is Annie, your beautiful wife?"

"Thank-you for asking. She's fine! I'll tell her that you asked."

Wang ushered Harry and Dr. Angus to a booth for four at the secluded end of the restaurant. It was clearly a location where a private conversation could take place.

"Harry must be about to disclose something to us that he wants to remain confidential," Angus concluded.

They were barely seated when Wang appeared leading Fr. Leo and Canon Matthew to their booth. Harry and Dr. Angus stood and greeted them warmly.

"So glad that you could make it, gentlemen. I know that it was short notice, but I need your advice on two matters today. But first, let's order our lunch."

After checking with his guests as to what were their favourite Chinese dishes, Harry called over the waitress and placed an order for eight dishes from the dim sum menu. Everyone agreed that they favoured jasmine tea, so he included a large pot with the order.

As they waited for their meals to arrive, they engaged in animated conversation, reminiscing about how their joint efforts with the other ten clerics had changed the town's perception of Christianity in the community, acknowledging that not everyone was pleased with the new found influence the coalition was having. No one was interested in dessert following the meal, and the waitress cleared their table.

Harry began. "What I'm about to say to you is strictly confidential. You are each a close friend. Annie and I have been discussing two major but unrelated concerns which I want now to drop into your laps. Please, after you hear of them, be perfectly honest in telling me whether they make sense or not."

"We're all ears, Harry," responded Fr. Leo. "What's got you two so fired up?"

"Well, the first is really perhaps a personal matter, but one that I feel needs to be considered. You all know that over the past few years my life has dramatically taken a turn for the better - a turn that at one time in the past I could never have even imagined would happen – that is, my baptism and becoming a committed Christian.

"There is a special person who planted the seeds of my conversion journey, now my great friend, The Rev. Canon Dr. Barkley Steadmore. As you are well aware, he and Faith no longer live in Tangleville. He's retired. But it was he who was really responsible for the incredible formation of the Tangleville Coalition.

You will remember, it all started with two quotes on my radio show. Dr. Steadmore made a statement that really caused me to think. Perhaps you were listening at the time, but he said "If you were ever accused of being a Christian, would there be enough evidence to convict you?"

"I remember him saying that," interjected Fr. Leo. "It really struck! In fact, I used it in a sermon the following Sunday."

"I remember it as well," chimed in Canon Matthew, "for he quoted that line in a sermon at St. Bart's the Sunday before your show. He was the guest preacher of the day."

"But...," continued Harry, "the statement he followed up with was the line that jolted me into calling you, Dr. Angus. The statistic he gave back then claimed that present day Christianity is subdivided into over 32,000 plus different denominations, with more being added every day. I was shocked! I asked myself, was Jesus so vague in his three year ministry that his followers could so differ in trying to interpret what he taught?"

"You remember that call I made to you Dr. Angus. I was so excited that you were willing to talk with me about those quotes. And, the rest is history! The Tangleville Christian Coalition was formed. The Tangleville Christian Manifesto followed. Now, two years later, our Christian presence in our town in no longer fractured. We are a community united in our public presence. We 'stepped out' together to challenge the secular status quo!"

"I remember that all so well, Harry," replied Dr. Angus. "At first I was certain that you were up to one of your old tricks or trying to manoeuvre a cleric into accepting a risky guest appearance on your radio show. But when you wanted to come over to my office, you really threw me. I asked myself, what were you up to? Yes, I remember it well!"

Harry continued. "Annie and I think that somehow Dr. Steadmore ought to be honoured for being the catalyst in what is now our united Christian presence in town. But we are lost as to how to go about doing so - indeed, if it ought to be done at all. We need your advice. What do you think? Are we way off base?"

"I'm all for it," chimed in Fr. Leo. "It is long overdue!"

"I agree," replied Canon Matthew. "But you have to recognise that I am his personal friend. I replaced him at St. Bart's where he is still loved and highly spoken of. What really needs to be done is to consult the other ten clerics of the coalition and see how they feel about the matter. But you have my vote."

Dr. Angus, always the wise and practical thinker suggested: "Why don't we recommend to the coalition that an award - an annual award - be established with the first being conveyed on Steadmore? Then, each year, we can honour an individual who for the past twelve months has been judged worthy of outstanding service to the Christian Church in town. That way it can become an annual occurrence! We could call it 'The Christian Disciple of the Year Award.' I'd be most willing to see that such an item be put on the agenda when we all meet on at our next Wednesday meeting. As you know, the next meeting will be taking place at St. Andrew's, and I will of course be chairing the event."

It was unanimous. The twelve clerics would have their say.

Then Harry dropped a bomb shell into the laps of his closely trusted friends. Taking a deep breath, followed by a lengthy pause, he said, "I'm also thinking seriously of letting my name stand on the ballot for the upcoming election for town council: ward three, the ward in which Annie and I reside. This is why I need your advice today. Should I do it? Would it help the Christian cause if I should be elected to town council? Will the coalition approve of my running for election?"

The announcement took the three clerics completely by surprise. There was a long pause. Dr. Angus broke the silence: "Tangleville desperately needs a person of faith on council who is not afraid to be labelled as being not politically correct. I don't know of anyone who fits the bill better than you, Harry. Go for it!"

All three clerics rose to their feet, and one after the other, shook Harry's hand. It was a gesture of affirmation that Harry needed to receive. He could hardly wait to tell Annie.

He thanked his guests and asked each to pray for God's guidance in the matter. He picked up the bill for the meal, and on the plate were four fortune cookies.

"You'd better read yours," teased Fr. Leo. "Your answer to run as a candidate might be wrapped up in a roll of dough."

Harry cracked open the fortune cookie and read it to his friends: "Your future lies in a stepping out discussion this day."

The four laughed uproariously.

EPILOGUE

HENRY Ford once said, "Coming together is a beginning, staying together is progress and working together is success." Thomas Stallkamp put it another way: "The secret is to gang up on the problem, rather than each other." The Tangleville Christian Coalition, now in its fifth year of existence, has more than proven that these two quotes can change the status quo.

Canon Dr. Steadmore's first guest appearance on the Harry Sting Show six years ago sowed the seeds of untangling Tangleville's competing Christian denominations when Harry asked the question, "Why is it such a problem that Christianity is so divided?

Steadmore replied, quoting from our Lord's prayer to His Father, the words of St. John , Chapter 17, verse 21: *"I ask not only on behalf of these (his apostles), but also on behalf of those who will believe in me through their word, that they may be one."*

Steadmore then made the statement that so resonated with Tangleville's Christian clerical members and the laity from the various denominational churches: "Today we are a long, long way, as Christians, from being one in Christ."

Little did Harry Sting realize at that time of his luncheon date with the Reverend Doctor Angus McLaughlin at the Samaritan Inn how God was at work. For from such a seemingly mundane gathering, the words of Jack Cranfield were again verified. Cranfield had said:

"One individual can begin a movement that turns the tide of history. Martin Luther King in the civil rights movement, Mohandas Gandhi of India, and Nelson Mandela in South Africa are examples of people standing up with courage and non-violence to bring about changes."

As a result of that meeting, secularism was about to be challenged in Tangleville. Four years later an untangling mechanism was firmly established within the Christian communities. It took the willingness of the twelve Christian denominations to step out together as the Body of Christ in trust with never-before explored co-operative milestones.

At first there was scepticism and fear expressed by the non-Christian members of the town as the movement was initially grossly misunderstood. Many feared that a united Christian voice would be an attempt to coerce non-believers into becoming converts to the faith, that their secular freedoms would be curtailed, depriving them of lifestyle choices currently permissible by law.

Some claimed that the intention of the Christian Coalition was a political movement whose sole purpose was to reverse the time cherished concept of separation of church and state. Slowly, their fears subsided when they began to grasp the broad meaning of Stepping Out, the slogan which the united Christians expressed in every possible way.

Stepping Out, they soon discovered, meant the end of internal Christian in-fighting where the different Christian denominations criticized each other's theology and a beginning of socializing together and cooperating in each other's social and charitable outreach programs to demonstrate God's love.

It became evident that the preferred styles of liturgies practiced by the various denominations were not issues to be debated. What was soon obvious was that the Christians were intent on non-compliance with society's norms and activities which were scheduled to interfere with worship times on Sundays.

No longer was the town's community focusing on Roman Catholics, Presbyterians, Baptists, Anglicans - indeed the various denominations - as separate competing faith communities, but now all were observed as a collective presence known simply as 'the Christians', but before, when a denomination spoke for or against some aspect of current society, it could be merely written off as one dissatisfied but squeaky wheel. Now such collective voices of dissent could not be dismissed. The Christians were now a united voice speaking at large, too many in number to simply ignore.

Most importantly, the power of stepping out was slowly grasped by the town to mean selective non-compliance by the Christian community, saying 'no' passively and non-violently, withdrawing their support for secular activities which they considered as non-scriptural. Passive resistance was becoming the key to being taken seriously in the town.

It soon became obvious that Christians were no longer shopping in droves on Sunday. Hence, Sunday shopping was becoming an issue for shopkeepers. Was it good business practice to hire staff for such reduced commercial enterprises? Staff deserved a day of rest as well.

The Christians were now organizing their own sporting activities for youth at times which did not conflict with worship hours. If fundraising events were scheduled to conflict with hours of worship on Sundays, the Christians refused to take part. Usually participating at a later date raised more dollars than the original secular events. This was being noticed by both groups! What did it all mean?

The Christians simply answered their critics by repeating words of a country song made famous by Lorrie Morgan, the phrase, "What part of 'no' don't you understand?" In other words, "we are not telling you what to do, or how to live your life - we are simply saying no to the aspects of secularism which we don't find are compatible with Christian theology."

And this applies as well for all religious faiths within our culture. All faiths, Muslims, Jews, Buddhists, etc., have the right to object, the right to think otherwise from the status quo of secular religion. Passive, non-aggressive non-compliance is a fundamental essential freedom of a true democracy whenever the laws of the land are not violated. After all, as religious practitioners argue: "Secularism is a modern competing religion with all the others. Why should this one religion dominate while attempting to silence those who differ?"

Perhaps the most notable change within Tangleville was the emergence of public demonstrations of Christian festivals in which all the twelve denominations participated. It took considerable effort on the part of the coalition to persuade the town council into granting permits to do so. Secular society does not readily grant permits to religious organizations to hold public events. However, with councillors now fully aware of a united Christian presence in town, it was politically expedient to make exceptions to a voting block that could determine councillors' victory or defeat in future elections. Political correctness has its political price! Ever so progressively, the Christians were availing themselves of the power of collaboration just as Ryunosuhe Satoro phrased it, "Individually, we are a drop. Together, we are an ocean."

Consequently, permits were reluctantly granted and the Christians seized the opportunity to become more visible than they had in the past as single denominations. They organized .The live Christmas crèche setting in the town park was another perfect example. Live animals were brought in from country farms by rural adherents. Lighting was set up by qualified volunteer electricians, with a large bright artificial star beaming down on the manger setting, the star visible for blocks around. Background music was provided to set the mood of the holy portrayal. Each year the Tangleville Mirror covered the event in detail, the occasion becoming so popular that even non-church people brought their children just to pet the animals.

Easter Sunday, however, became the annual major co-operative exhibition of Christian witness in town - an Ecumenical Easter Sunrise Prayer Service with all twelve clergy participating in the liturgy. Following the early ecumenical gathering individual congregations then celebrated their particular style of Easter Services in their own parish settings. The message to the secular culture was clear: Easter is the celebration of the resurrection of Christ, the Son of God. Not one bunny rabbit nor one Easter egg would make an appearance!

For those who knew their New Testament, the words of St. Paul were being put into practice when he wrote in the letter to the Ephesians, 4:16: *"But speaking the truth in love, we must grow up in every way into him who is the head, into Christ, from whom the whole body, joined and knitted together by every ligament with which it is equipped, as each part is working properly, promotes the body's growth in building itself up in love."*

Now, working together, major concerns of the Christian faith could be addressed in a far more productive fashion than if individual denominations attempted to do so on their own. These concerns were legion: help for the homeless, the sharing of resources through the Might of the Mite Fund, refugee resettlements, abuse and abortion, violence, cruelty, housing projects, combatting the spread of pornography, the establishment of youth projects - teamwork was the key to success.

Charles Darwin said, "It is the long history of humankind (and animal kind too) that those who learned to collaborate and improvise most effectively have prevailed." Perhaps, though, Vince Lombardi put it best: "Individual commitment to a group effort – that's what makes a team work, a company work, a society work, a civilization work."

To their great credit, Tangleville's Christians were finally acknowledging that the body of Christ is comprised of one body with many members. St. Paul centuries ago, attempted to state this fact, when he wrote in his First Letter to the Corinthians, 12:12, 15-20:

> "For just as the body is one and has many members, and all the members of the body, though many are one body, so it is with Christ. If the foot were to say 'because I am not a hand, I do not belong to the body', that would not make it any less a part of the body. And if the ear were to say, 'because I am not any eye, I do not belong to the body', that would not make it any less a part of the body. If the whole body were an eye, where would the hearing be? If the whole body were hearing, where would the sense of smell be? But as it is, God arranged the members in the body, each one of them, as he chose. If all were a single member, where would the body be? As it is, there are many members, yet one body."

Bit by bit, together, the Christians were slowly but surely untangling Tangleville's secular religious hold on its town's folk. They had learned that Harvey Cox was correct when he wrote, "Secularism is not only indifferent to alternative religious systems, but as a religious ideology it is opposed to any other religious systems. It is therefore a closed system."

It is a fact that time turns the past into revision. Tangleville had changed along with its individual citizens. Audrey Holmes was a prime example as she moved on following the death of her beloved Jack. It was a emotional time for her following the funeral. For twelve months she found it difficult to pursue activities outside her home, other than attending church at St. Bart's and doing her grocery shopping and banking. It was only when her best friend Claire called inviting her to attend a play at the downtown theatre, that she finally felt up to attending a social event. As a result, sitting next to her was a gentleman she had never met. Informal introductions followed. They agreed to meet on the following Wednesday for coffee at the Bean Grinder. A year and a half later, Audrey became the spouse of Doctor James Barker, a widower whose wife had passed away three years earlier. It was a new life for both!

Doctor Angus McLaughlin announced to his congregation that he would be retiring next year at the end of June. He and Lois were planning a four-month cruise around the world, and then settling into retirement in a condo in Tangleville. Dr. Angus would continue to write his weekly column in the Tangleville Mirror and work with the coalition after he retired.

Father Leo Mahoney was promoted to the rank of Monsignor with administrative duties extending throughout the diocese. Tangleville, however, remained special in his memory of all the various parishes he had served. When the Bishop bestowed the title upon him, Fr. Leo, by special invitation, requested that the other eleven clerical members of the Tangleville Christian Coalition and their spouses, along with Harry Sting and Annie, be present at the liturgy. All attended.

A new priest, Father Michael Scanlan was appointed to replace Dr. Leo at St. Anne's. He immediately requested membership in the Tangleville Christian Coalition clergy group.

The secretarial staff at the twelve churches continue to meet for lunch on a monthly basis, exchanging ideas for co-operation in areas of social activities, outreach and charitable assistance to the community. They have been invaluable in recruiting volunteers from within their parish communities to assist at the ever-expanding Samaritan Inn, now a two structure campus totalling one hundred and seventy rooms, one residence for males and another for females in recovery mode.

Jim and Judy Sallow have fully reconciled with their once-ostracised daughter Joy, son-in-law Art, and granddaughter. The relationship which was strained for years has now been healed, with Jim and Judy becoming doting grandparents, attempting to make up for those years of rejecting their own. Art now has a new, well-paying job, but Jim and Judy still continue to generously bestow gifts of financial support to all three.

Jim donated his Dodge Ram 4x4 to Art, and purchased a new Ford Explorer 4x4 for Judy and himself. There still, beneath the surface, lurks a sense of guilt for their former behaviour, but time is slowly healing the past! They have even come around to the approving of Father Claybourne's high Anglican liturgy!

Lefty Jones was now a local hero. He continues to organize sporting events for youth as well as adults. Two adult baseball teams under his guidance, have risen to the level where they now play against other neighbouring Christian teams in surrounding local towns. In an exhibition game against the Tangleville Turbos, the Tangleville Templars defeated the official team by a score of 6 to 1. Of course, the Turbos tried to recruit some of the Templars' best players, but each player who was enticed to join their team, refused, stating that they didn't want to play if it would mean interference with Sunday worship and family time.

The highlight of the year had become the annual Christian Family Picnic gathering in the Tangleville park. Numbers were growing every year since that dunking tank auction raising money for the Samaritan Inn. The event attracted parishioners from all twelve denominations in the town, as well as many non-church goers whose children, upon hearing about the great food, games and fun events, coerced their parents to take them to the event. Many of their friends from their elementary and secondary school classes were church goers, and hearing of the great times of the gathering, wanted to attend as well. The annual event became a recruiting tool for Lefty who oversaw the baseball games during each picnic.

Barclay and Faith were invited to attend the most recent picnic, unaware of why they were so passionately urged to do so. They, not suspecting the real reason for their invitation, were overwhelmed when Harry Sting, during the midst of the after luncheon announcements, called the two to the microphone. Immediately Barclay suspected that it was going to be his turn in the dunking machine to be auctioned off by the Rev. Charles McCormick as a money making event to raise funds for the Samaritan Inn. To his complete surprise, Harry announced that The Rev. Canon Dr. Barclay Steadmore was to be honoured as the first recipient of The Christian Disciple of the Year Award for outstanding service to the Ecumenical Christian Churches in town.

Barclay and Faith were completely lost for words. Faith could not control her tears of surprise, and Barclay just managed to stay dry-eyed.

The crowd burst into a hearty round of congratulatory applause and Barclay, somewhat controlling his emotions, thanked the gathering for this, as he put it, "undeserved honour." He was told that his was the first of many future recipient names to be placed on the trophy.

The Tangleville Mirror reporter present amongst the crowd, snapped the picture of Barclay, Faith, and Harry and the lead story in Monday's edition featured the picture of the three along with a full coverage of the day's activities. Faith claimed that if they had known that she and Barclay were to be so honoured, they would have worn dressier clothes. It was though, she admitted, a great picture!

On their way back to their home in Trinity Harbour, the top down on their Mustang convertible, Faith and Barclay reminisced over how their lives had unfolded together. Barclay, in paraphrased fashion, quoted to Faith the words of Carl Jung from his work *Memories, Dreams, Reflections*: "As far as we can discern, the sole purpose of human existence is to kindle a light in the darkness of mere being."

"That light, Faith, has to be the light of Christ! Our Lord has blessed us beyond measure, don't you agree?"

Faith reached over and squeezed his hand. That's all she needed to do. Words were not necessary.

Two weeks later, Harry, with Annie at his side, held a news conference with representatives present from the Tangleville Mirror and AM KNOW. "I'm letting my name stand for election as town councillor in ward three in the oncoming election this fall"

Harry was immediately inundated with questions from the reporters and attempted to answer them truthfully and individually. One reporter's question would set the theme for Harry's success or failure in winning the seat. It would define his campaign, and if elected, how he on council would represent his constituents.

"Mr. Sting, how are you intending to differentiate yourself from all the others during the campaign, and if you are elected, on council?"

Without hesitation Harry replied, "I'm going to remain true to my Christian convictions and not be 'stung' by secular political correctness!"

Harry turned toward his spouse and winked. Annie smiled. She understood completely.

Donald H. Hull, D. Min.

CPSIA information can be obtained
at www.ICGtesting.com
Printed in the USA
BVOW08*0945191217
503201BV00003B/5/P